I Will Have You!

By
Gena Kinder

PublishAmerica
Baltimore

© 2006 by Gena Kinder.
All rights reserved. No part of this book may be reproduced, stored in a retrieval system or transmitted in any form or by any means without the prior written permission of the publishers, except by a reviewer who may quote brief passages in a review to be printed in a newspaper, magazine or journal.

First printing

All characters appearing in this work are fictitious. Any resemblance to real persons, living or dead, is purely coincidental.

ISBN: 1-4241-5089-2
PUBLISHED BY PUBLISHAMERICA, LLLP
www.publishamerica.com
Baltimore

Printed in the United States of America

Dedication

I would like to dedicate this book to my two children, Kyia and Cordell. For without their patience and support I would never have finished. I would also like to thank my parents CJ and Charlanna for their unwavering confidence in me. I love you all and thank you.

Chapter 1

"You ungrateful bastard. I should have left you with that whore of a mother on the streets where I found you," William Morris shouted as he stomped up the stairs. Anger welled up inside of him, ready to spill over. His eyebrows slid down, causing angry creases to wrinkle up his already blotched features. Jeff had always been a disappointment as a son. William could not understand why he had no interest in becoming financially stable. As he, himself, searched for riches and security for his family. His son had become a lawyer and a Union sympathizer. In a time when war was breaking out everywhere, he had a turncoat in his own house. Damn the war and damn the president. Why couldn't everything just stay the same?

William Morris knew he was a shrewd, self-made, ambitious man who never allowed anything or anyone to get in his way. He would have and has thrown his friends to the vultures when the need arose. His hard working, business orientated mind had been successful in assisting him to weasel his way into the endless money pockets of those sniveling fools he called boss. The last unexpected victim he had worked for was John Gram. Mr. Gram had become a personal miracle to William. Gram believed himself to be a financial genius, even though railways were his only source of income. Which to William, that was very idiotic. Always have a backup company. Mr. Gram thought he was secure though, because he owned over a quarter of all the railways that spread from Maine to North Carolina. The new branch was suppose to stretch from the mountains of Tennessee to California.

Mr. Gram was trying to purchase the Northwest Railways. The present owner was on the verge of filing bankruptcy and was very agreeable about selling. William knew there was promise in this. Mr. Gram always said using migrant under paid workers to do all the labor was profitable, all you had to do is sit back and reap the rewards. The ramifications of their use were unfathomable. Profits would just build up. With the war progressing and the need to transport soldiers to their needed locations grew, so did the idea of profiting from it.

During the legal proceedings, Gram introduced William as his partner on this deal. He gave William the full control of the funds and legal documents to back up the claim. The proceedings were going perfect, when Mr. Gram died. The cause was never identified, so the coroner ruled it natural causes. With the boss dead, this left William to seal the deal in his name, thus becoming the newest railroad owner in the divided country.

To help his new empire to grow, William purchased some land in the Northwest Territories. It was not exactly to his liking because of all the savages still running loose on the land. Fortunately for him the government was rounding them up and placing them on reservations. Other than that, the land would be very easy to manipulate. It was nothing more than a dust bowl anyways. William was a determined man and all that really concerned him was to finish laying the five-hundred miles of track before winter. It would be the first to reach to California. It was to be the greatest undertaking for the railway industries.

William watched his underpaid and overworked men slave away for him and he received great satisfaction from it. Dreams are what

I WILL HAVE YOU!

the future held and his dreams have always been about riches. Every time he added new tracks to his dreams it was luscious, but on the particular job it was honey for the bear. Scanning over the crowd, William noticed a group of worker standing in a circle, just staring at the ground. As he went to investigate, his foreman Paul stepped away from the group and approached him.

"Sir," Paul shouted excitedly, "the ground is bleeding!" William stepped into the circle of men to survey the ground. OIL, oil was oozing out of the ground. William was not a man to show emotion, but a smile crept across his face.

"Paul, block off this area. I will be back as soon as possible." Paul looked up giving a puzzled look.

"Where are you going sir?" William looked back with a cock-eyed grin.

"To file the papers on my new claim, what else." With that said, he walked away.

William had decided to put this new venture into his son's name. After all, he had fallen in love with the railroads and as much as the oil business brought in money, his new passion would be fine with him. He would always have it to fall back on. He knew he had not been much of a father to Jeff in the last five years and he wanted to rectify this. He just wasn't prepared for his son's refusal.

"Me, an ungrateful bastard. You're the bastard," Jeff Morris shouted back as he followed him up the stairs. "You never asked me if I wanted it. You only assumed you knew best. I do not want hand outs from you. My mother and I were of no concern to you, why should you care now?"

"Your mother was never a concern to me. She was nothing but a whore. But you are my son and will keep the wealth in the family. My name will carry on." Jeff finally reached the top of the stairs and reached out, forcefully spinning William around to face him.

"You leave my mother out of this. No concern of yours, ha. You left her alone to fend for herself and me. No money, No food. She did what she had to do."

"Your mother would have still been with us if she hadn't whored around," William said, his eyes blazing with anger. "I have wished so many times to turn back the clocks. Hoping you had froze to death that night outside of that door. My mistake was coming back for my family, period."

Waves of rage surged through Jeff. He clenched his fists at his side, holding his anger in check as he turned around, putting his back towards his father. "You have no right to talk about me, or about my mother that way," Jeff ground out between clenched teeth. William looked at Jeff's white knuckles before he stepped around him and confronted him face to face.

Noticing a glimpse of tears in Jeff's eyes, William started to laugh in Jeff's face. "What are you going to do, huh? Strike me or cry? What's on your mind? Do it, cry baby." Jeff raised his clenched fist up as William ground his forehead into Jeff's. "Do it coward!" Letting the laughter fade William backed up from Jeff. "I knew you couldn't do it," he stated matter of fact. "You weak, lazy, inconsiderate bastard. Get out of my sight. As of today my foreman Paul will inherit everything, the oil, the railroads and yes, this very house along with the fortune." William began to laugh again. Jeff couldn't tell if his father was losing his mind or just messing with him. Regardless the reason, the thought of losing all the money was not to his liking.

"You can't do that, I'm your son and I have all rights to take over everything you own," Jeff shouted stabbing William's chest with his finger. William looked at his son, not caring anymore.

"As of right now you are no longer my son. I am changing my will as of today. You will be a pauper."

That's all Jeff could take. Raising both of his arms up he shoved his father hard in the chest. "You are the reason my mother is dead." One more shove pushed him another step backwards. "You drove her to do what she did." Another shove. "You abandoned us." And another. By now the heals of Williams boots were balanced precariously at the top ledge of the stairwell. Jeff sneered, taking a step closer to the source of his anger. "And you have never meant anything to me except room service," Jeff whispered as he gave one final shove.

Williams's heart skipped a beat as his body lurched backwards. He frantically tried to reach for the banister, but the well polished rail forced his fingertips to slip off as the weight of his body toppled downwards. William twisted his body around to try and stop his fall, but instead he only succeeded to angle his body perfectly so that his head thrust between the railing posts of the third and fourth steps.

Jeff, seeing that his father was trapped stepped down and leaned over the rail to stare into his father's eyes. "Do you know the difference between you and I?" Jeff replied, "I don't use a gun." With that Jeff kicked his fathers badly positioned feet with his own well polished boots. A loud cracking sound echoed through the hall. Jeff peered down at the grotesque sight. Williams's neck bones were protruding through the torn skin. The beautifully tanned carpet turned a dark red and blood seeped down the white wash stairwell. Jeff had never witnessed the gross distortion of a human body before. The scene kept him in entranced for a few moments. Then the thought of someone coming in snapped his mind back to the present. Jeff gingerly walked down the remaining steps, pausing long enough to kick a lifeless foot out of his way. That was that, he was now free. Jeff hummed a merry tune as he walked out the door.

Chapter 2

"So, Congressman Sanders. I hear you're running for the Governorship," inquired Charles Hubbard as he sat back in the new leather plush chair.

"You heard correct, Sergeant Hubbard. I believe that Governor Francis Pickers needs some competition," Jonathan stated as he arose and walked around the desk to the bookcases. "I believe I will have the advantage also." Jon walked his finger from book-to-book till he reached out and removed a large, leather bound book and handed it to Charles.

Glancing at the cover, Charles read out loud. "Medical Journal." Charles' features narrowed into a frown. "I don't understand. What does a book of medicine have to do with politics?"

"Don't you see, Charles?" he exclaimed most excitedly. "Look, think about it."

Jonathan stood up and turned around and opened the stained glass window that was perched behind his desk. "Look out there, what do you see?"

I WILL HAVE YOU!

Charles stood up, his gaze locked on the open window as he approached. Peering outside of City Hall, he scanned the few blocks that were directly in his sight. A few carriages were traveling down the finely cobbled roads. Towns folk were shopping and enjoying the warm day. Even a small dog ran across the adjoining street barking and chasing pigeons. "I see nothing out of the ordinary, Jon. Is there a point to this?" Jon blinked his eyes a few times in astonishment, it was perfectly clear to him.

"Charles, the Governor put this town under quarantine four years ago when a plague attacked this town," Jon stated.

"You mean I've been trapped here for three months because of a scare four years ago!" Charles hung his head and began to laugh.

"It wasn't a scare, Charles. Town's people started dying by the dozens. Dr. Jeninson sent telegraphs out asking for help from anyone that would listen," Jon said as he ran his fingers through his brown shoulder length hair.

"A doctor...ooh I can't remember his name right now, but he sent back word that with the symptoms...and the time it took to kill its victims and the unknown way it spread. He said it was possibly Bubonic Plague. That's all it took for the Governor to close our town to outsiders. No one came in and no one out."

Jon wiped his brow. Just telling what happened brought back memories. His wife and his three year old daughter had succumbed to the sickness. He still wonders why he was cursed to live. Watching his family pass away and then having to watch as they were carried away to be burned was the most horrific event in his thirty years.

"Was it ever confirmed?" Charles asked as he opened the book and flipped through the pages with keen interest.

"No, no it wasn't," Jon said looking up at Charles. "But, I hope to change that. If I want to be Governor, this quarantine has to be eliminated. It's been a year and a half since the last body was destroyed. You would think that the Governor would have cleared the town by now." Jon let out a deep sigh. "It's as if the whole world has left us to rot. You, Charles, are the first and probably the last person that will come to this town."

"You just may be right, Jon. I received a telegram from my unit. Apparently coming here ruined my career. My commander sent word that I'm no longer a sergeant in the Confederate Army. The circumstances of the quarantine also spread by word of mouth to the other units, both Union and ours. No one is permitted near this town." Charles looked up at the sky. "I'm stuck here along with all of you, aren't I?"

"I'm afraid so. We cannot travel more than fifty miles in any direction. We slowly starve to death because we have to rely on what we grow and make. But I plan on fixing all this and that book is the key," Jon replied as he gestured towards the book that was still in Charles' hands.

Jon watched as Charles' expression changed from nonchalant to a grim smile. He knew Charles wanted to go home and he also knew that would probably never happen. Charles and two other soldiers found their way to Oak Ridge in South Carolina, purely by accident. Apparently, they had been ambushed by Union sympathizers while transporting supplies to Charleston Harbor. The attack was swift and brutal. All but Charles and two privates were able to get away, unfortunately they all had injuries. Charles had taken a musket ball in the arm and the other two had bayonet wounds to their chests.

The wounded men were able to locate a mount that only had superficial injuries. Charles was able to secure a gurney to the animal and transported the two soldiers and guided the animal through the woods. After traveling for two days, the town that came into sight was very welcome. Sadly the two soldiers died from their wounds a few days later. Most of the towns officials had visited Charles and had become fast friends during his healing. It was a bittersweet occasion, considering it was the first company they'd had in years.

Jon knew that Charles had sent off the telegram to his company while he was healing. If he finally received an answer back that means that it took three months to come full circle. "I am so sorry Charles," Jon said. "You know if we can get the quarantine lifted, they may take you back."

"From what you tell me that would be a marvelous accomplishment, if it can be done," Charles said as he glanced out the window again. Everyone looked so healthy. How can this still be going on? He needed to get out of this town. His career stood in the balance. "If there is anything that I can do to help, I will. You know that."

"Well you know that Dr. Jeninson is helping with this also. I think with his first hand knowledge we will be able to beat this." Jon leaned his head against the side of the window. "Charles, do you know any doctor's out there that can help?" Jon paused but no answer came forth. "Charles?" Again no answer. Jon looked over at Charles. Charles looked as if he was going to fall out of the window. Jon followed Charles' gaze out the window and a low chuckle escaped his lips. There down below was a lovely young lady. She was wearing a stunning spring green gown with a white shawl. She was so graceful and appeared to be extra careful with everything she looked at. Charles stared as she picked up different items, looked them over and set them back down.

"You definitely have an eye. She is very beautiful. Why don't you go and introduce yourself." Jon noticed the smile that creased his companions' lips. "We'll talk later when I have more news."

"Thank you, Jon," he said as he raced towards the door. "I'll inform you of what happens also…bye, Jon." Charles gave a final backwards glance and winked as he left the office. Jon laughed quietly to himself as he watched Charles sprint down the road after the young heart catcher. He turned away from the window and lifted the book up from where Charles had left it and started his studies once more.

Chapter 3

"Oh, how lovely," Monica exclaimed as she lifted a delicate porcelain figure of a women into her hands. It reminded Monica of her mother. Very frail with long blonde hair, rosy cheeks and a sparkle in her blue eyes. The figure of the women seemed to be knitting a scarf. Her mother never knitted, but it still resembled her. Tears welled up in her eyes as she visualized her mother.

It had been two years since she passed away from the sickness. She was only seventeen when her mother developed a red rash with small bumps that spread all over her body. Soon after, her body was engulfed by fever. She would sit by her mother, dabbing her heated skin with wet clothes. Hoping that she would just wake up. She never did. It only took three days for the illness to run its course and take her mothers' life with it. Her father followed no more than a week later along with half of her friends.

The towns officials said it was easier to burn the bodies in the caves between Sandersonville and Oak Ridge. The towns were only five miles away from each other which put her little home in risk along with everyone else.

I WILL HAVE YOU!

As she wiped away the tears, she carried the fragile figure to the shopkeeper. "I'll take this one," Monica said as she paid for her precious memory and left. She decided to continue her shopping since it was so lovely a spring day. It called to her, drawing her outside, making her giddy. She glided down the street, taking a few moments here and there to peer into different shops. She was staring into the dressmakers shop to view a bright blue gown that was so low cut in the chest area it made her blush. Who would wear that? It was simply scandalous. Monica was stepping back from the window when the reflection of a gentleman caught her attention.

Monica turned slightly as not to be noticed looking back in return. Her eyes met the most erotic sight she had ever seen. A well dressed gentleman stood there, across the street from her, staring as if in a trance. Eyes, that were so bright blue peered at her. They were like sapphires, so intense. It seemed like time stood still as their gazes locked for a few moments. A group of excited springtime shoppers walked between them, breaking the connection between them.

Monica blinked a few times, trying to get her bearings back. It took a few seconds for her to realize that she had dropped the basket she had been carrying. She bent down to pick it up and when she stood back up, he was gone. A twinge of sadness crept over her. She turned and looked in all directions hoping to catch another glimpse of the handsome stranger, but to no avail. He was gone.

She quickly composed herself and brushed away the odd feeling's that had welled up inside of her. *He could not have seen me*, she thought to herself as she turned onto Bayberry St. She took one more glance over her shoulder before continuing her day. As she walked down the road away from Maine St. a sweet aroma filled her senses. It was the aromatic smell of freshly baked bread. She looked around until she found the one place it would have come from. "Bakery and Deli" the sign read as she entered the building.

A tiny bell rang out from above her head as she opened the door, then rang out a second time as the door closed behind her. She was only able to take a few steps into the store. There were numerous shoppers of all ages filed along the well stocked shelves. Looking around, she noticed that all sorts of goods were sold in here. By her legs were boxes marked "Cheese" along with an assortment list. Along the wall shelves were flour, salt, sugar, and dried meats. On the other side of the room were barrels marked "Pickles." There were so many things that one could get spoiled in here. At least she had plenty of time to decide.

The bell sounded off again as a customer left the bakery, allowing Monica to move up some more. An area finally opened up that allowed her to view the counter. Her eye's shifted from one person to another. She just couldn't decide what to purchase. Everything smelled so delectable that her mouth started to water. One lady had a few Queen Ann rolls. Another had a loaf of fresh baked bread. Monica noticed that the bakery also sold a variety of fresh meats and cheeses. The gentleman at the counter was carefully picking out an assortment, taking free samples as he chose them. He would shake his head one way or the other depending on what he tasted. He was being very picky.

Monica inhaled a startled breath when the gentleman turned to pick out a new picnic basket from the top shelf. It was him. Her palms became sweaty and she could feel her heart rate speed up. She just stood there watching him as he shook his head in approval of his purchases. His shoulder length hair waved gracefully up and then down. Not one strand of hair moved out of place. She was so close that she could smell his cologne he was wearing. The smell was very pleasing to her senses.

She allowed her eye's to scan over his entire body, appreciating the sight. He was dressed in a gray waistcoat with tails that hung down to his knees. Perfectly pressed black slacks could be seen from below the tails and the collar of a crisp white dress shirt could be seen peaking of the top of the high collar of the matching gray dress jacket.

Without warning he turned around. Her heart fled into her throat and blushed. It was shameful the way she reacted to him. She went to leave before he could see her. She turned with such force, that she knocked over an old pickle barrel. A wave of relief flooded over her when she realized that it was still capped. Thankfully not one drop leaked from the enormous wooden container.

I WILL HAVE YOU!

A frightened gasp escaped her lips. The sound was so short and high pitched that it amused Charles. He carefully set the picnic basket down and lifted the barrel back into an upright position with such ease that it astonished his lovely admirer. He took only a moment to rest before turning to the lovely creature for whom he had already made plans. It amused him that she had found him. He didn't know if it was by accident or on purpose. It really didn't matter. She was here now.

Charles turned towards her and with a gentle calm, bowed and said, "Accidents are just that, accidents. Wouldn't you agree?" A grin was spread from cheek to cheek. It was so full of honest humor that Monica blushed again. The redness that came to her cheeks would have put the brightest rose to shame.

"Yes, but it can be very embarrassing to most people." They stood there for a few seconds, not knowing what else to say. Then Charles remembered his picnic basket. With a mischievous grin he bent over and retrieved it.

"A special lunch for a special lady?" Charles asked as he offered his arm. Seeing the hesitation Charles tried another approach. "It would be my pleasure if you were to join me for lunch." The phrase was stated such, that it was not a question but a begging demand. Monica was tempted to decline his offer, but another part of her raised and lowered her head in a compliant answer.

As they walked side by side, Monica studied the stranger who held her attention. This was not like her at all. She would never have gone with a stranger before. It was a little exciting because this would have normally been taboo. As they walked she studied this man that kept her attention. She could make out his well chiseled features and tanned skin. It looked as if he spent many hours out in the sun. His lips appeared to be set in a permanent smile. His high cheekbones only added to his perfect appearance. The only blemish on him was a tiny scar on his forehead. Even that only added to the mystery surrounding this man. It seemed so perfect to be next to him. She could not even explain these feelings to herself, but it felt right. Anything that felt this good could never be wrong.

Chapter 4

Mrs. Thomas had decided to wait for the doctor outside. The trauma of finding Mr. Morris was more than she could bare. It was not the first time she had seen a dead person, but the other one's had all died from disease or old age. This was neither of those causes. Her initial reaction was to scream, which alerted the rest of the people in the house. James, the driver, was the first to run in. What he saw made him stop in his tracks. He blocked the door as not to let Jenny see. She was so delicate, he didn't want her to witness anything this horrible. Jenny had been the cook in the house for five years now and James did not want her to see her boss like this.

Mrs. Morris remembered James dragging her out of the house and listened as he ordered that no one go back in until he returned with the sheriff. Her mind was in such a haze she did as she was told. Time seemed to pass so slowly, then when she was just about to give up the deputy showed up.

"The sheriff is investigating a horse robbery, so I have to handle this," he exclaimed.

"Where is James?" she inquired.

"I sent him for the doctor, he'll be here in a few minutes. Where is Mr. Morris?"

Mrs. Thomas got to her feet and pointed at the door. "He's in there on the stairs." Mrs. Thomas let the Deputy in but still did not reenter the house. Mrs. Thomas turned to watch the road as the deputy went inside and shut the door.

"Lord almighty!" Deputy Samuels exclaimed, followed by a loud whistle, as he looked over the distorted body of what was William Morris. Deputy Samuels had been born and raised in this town and about five years ago had become deputy. In all his twenty-seven years he had never seen such a grotesque sight. Pulling his night stick from it's holder on his utility belt, he carefully used it to lower the collar of Williams' shirt. It was so strange to see the back of the collar covering the chin of this once prominent man.

The skin of Williams neck resembled a corkscrew. It was all wrinkled and twisted towards the left. At least it looked like the left. Blood lined the creases, giving it a candy cane effect. Samuels closed his eyes and took a couple of much needed deep breaths before continuing. Standing up, he walked around the fresh corpse to the step above. He lodged the night stick under what he thought was the left shoulder and pressed down lightly to lift the shoulder a few inches off the step. He shifted the body only enough as to get a clear look at the laceration on the neck.

Blood had already started to coagulate on the skin, leaving a sticky residue on the ripped flesh. The skull bone could be clearly seen through an open gash above the ear. The backbone had been ripped from its normal position. This was evident since Williams' face and backbone were both facing the ceiling. The hardened deformity that was once his neck bone, looked as if it was positioned in his mouth like a sieve. When looking straight down it appeared as if William was sucking his own life's blood from himself like some demonic vampire.

John was still examining the corpse when the door at the bottom of the stairs burst open, distracting him. Without thinking, Samuels pressed down on his nightstick, which was still wedged underneath the shoulder, while rising. It raised Williams' shoulder up just enough for the body to shift. The remaining skin that held the corpses head in place separated, freeing the skull to fall away and allowing the torso to slide down the remaining stairs.

Mrs. Thomas was letting Dr. Mark Jeninson into the house when as an assortment of strange sounds reached their ears. They had taken no more than three steps into the house when Mrs. Thomas felt something bump her leg. The already traumatized women looked down at her feet and there, nestled between her two feet, was the head of William Morris staring up at her. A shock wave ravaged her body just before she lost all thought.

Dr. Jeninson tried to break her fall, but between his sixty-one years and her full figure, it was impossible to keep her upright. He watched in horror as her sliding feet kicked the decapitated skull back towards the stairs. Blood leaked out of the severed jugular veins, leaving odd shaped designs on the newly waxed floor.

"Deputy Samuels, if you wouldn't mind?" Dr. Jeninson asked as he looked up at him then back down at Mrs. Thomas. Samuels quickly descended the steps to where they were. Together, they half carried half dragged her limp body into the den. Being careful not to injure her, they lifted her up onto the davenport. Dr. Jeninson took a few moments to check her over. When he was sure that she would be all right, he motioned to Samuels for them to leave the room.

"Are you crazy?" Dr. Jeninson shouted angrily as they stepped into the hall, closing the door of the den behind them. "What were you thinking?"

Samuels looked down, pretending to admire the toe of his boots. "I was just looking, I've never…" A hand came up, silencing him.

"You know not to touch the bodies. That is my job," Dr. Jeninson said while running his fingers through his hair in frustration.

"I didn't see any harm in just looking at it."

"John Samuels, looking at it and what actually happened…" he said pointing at the severed head. "…are two different things. How am I suppose to rule on this one? Huh?" Dr. Jeninson asked as he stepped closer to the now-fumbled death scene.

"What do you mean, "rule"? It's purely a freak accident. Look around, what do you see?" Samuels said waving his hand through the air. "Nothing, no one was home."

"And how did you come to that conclusion?" Dr. Jeninson inquired sarcastically.

"I spoke with the driver on the way here. It seems that he and Mrs. Thomas and the cook Jenny had been in town picking up supplies. When they returned Mrs. Thomas found him." Samuels paused to take a quick breath.

"What about Jeff Morris? Where was he?" Dr. Jeninson interjected.

"I asked about him also."

"Well…"

"Apparently, on their return trip, all of them spotted Mr. Morris doing his daily ride in the fields. Before you ask, yes. This was a normal routine for Jeff." Samuels inputted.

"Was he coming from…or going towards town exactly?" Dr. Jeninson asked, frustration was setting in. Getting information from the Deputy was worse than trying to diagnose colic.

"From my understanding he was going in the direction of town." Dr. Jeninson rubbed his face with his hands. He would not be able to make hide nor hair out of the bumbled mess. This little bit of added information didn't appeal to him at all, but what could he do about it. You can't make a murder case without a weapon, signs of struggle or a witness. There was only one choice.

"John, we'll rule this an accident. I'll fill out the death certificate as such. While I'm making my notations, you go and find some sheets and cover this mess up."

Samuels went off to find the cook, Jenny. He hoped she would know where they were. It only took a few minutes to retrieve the requested items. Dr. Jeninson helped Samuels to spread the sheets over all of the blood spots and the deceased. No more than a few seconds after the sheets were down, they had absorbed the remaining blood that hadn't yet dried. Staining the sheets permanently.

"Why don't you go back to town and retrieve the grave man. I will stay and keep an eye on Mrs. Thomas while I wait for Mr. Jeff Morris to return."

Both men turned towards the door at the sound of a man's voice. "While you wait for who to return?"

Jeff Morris had heard the majority of the conversation between the two men in his house. They had been so occupied with covering his father's body, they had not noticed his return.

"Jeff…" Dr. Jeninson called out as he walked over to him. Jeff allowed himself to be guided back out the door. "I have to talk to you."

Samuels followed quietly behind. He had not had the opportunity to be introduced to Jeff as of yet, but he did notice that Jeff and the doctor were old friends. The easygoing manner in which they spoke with each other spoke volumes about their relationship. It didn't take Samuels long to realize that he wasn't needed. So, he took his leave in order to do his errands.

Jeff smiled to himself as he lifted the crystal decanter from the bar in the den and poured himself a much needed glass of brandy. The grave man had come and taken his father's body away. Mrs. Thomas had come to long enough for Dr. Jeninson to check her out and to give her a sedative to help her sleep. All of this seemed not to bother Jenny in the least. She was where she always is, in the kitchen cooking dinner and best of all, all of his unwanted guests were gone now. He couldn't believe it, he pulled everything off very neatly. The weeping, the tears, and the sorrow. Not too much though. After all, the doctor knew that he was not that close to his father. He didn't need to raise suspicion.

Raising the glass to his lips, Jeff swallowed the fiery liquid down in one gulp. Setting the glass down, Jeff leaned back onto *his* tulip printed, burgundy colored davenport. It was a new experience. *His*, that word had new meaning now. He couldn't believe that everything was his now. Unfortunately, that smile faded. There would be many things to do and places to go tomorrow. The funeral arrangements would have to be made. Then he would have to bring the family lawyer up to speed. Then he would finally search the house from attic to basement.

I WILL HAVE YOU!

There would be plenty of time for that since his main problem was going to be six feet under. Setting the empty glass down, Jeff coaxed his body into a lying position and allowed himself to slip into a peaceful sleep.

Chapter 5

    Monica and Charles strolled in silence for what seemed like eternity. He guided her to a little public square that overlooked the ocean. He chose a table that was just out of the eavesdropping range of the other people, but still within range of other's as not to make her uncomfortable. The last thing he wanted to do was to make her nervous. The truth being they were still strangers to each other, but still a trust for the other had ensued toward the other deep down inside of them.
    "Does this meet your expectations?" Charles asked. When no answer was forth coming he looked over at her. She appeared to be in her own world, peering around and looking at the wondrous sights. She had passed by, but had never stopped here. It was all so beautiful, she couldn't help but admire everything. The small stone tables were in perfect condition. They appeared to be made of red and brown stones in a sand mixture. She turned to her right where some pigeons were fighting for a few scraps of crumbs that lay on the ground. She spun to her left and there was a couple a few tables over, they were so

entranced with each other, they did not even notice when a stray pigeon flew up onto their table and stole a piece of pie crust before flying away again.

Hearing the crashing of waves, Monica turned around. She had not even noticed the ocean right there. It was so beautiful, not as beautiful as her shoreline, but still just as enchanting. The waves crashing in and gently receding always seemed so relaxing. A light breeze blew through her hair filling her senses with the smell of fresh salt water, which she inhaled deeply, letting the warm sensation it caused to roll over her body. *This felt so right,* she thought to herself. A low growl from a dog caught her attention, when she spun to find it, all she found was Charles' mid-section with her elbow.

"I asked if this would do?" he asked in a strained voice as he bent over holding his abdomen.

Monica stared at Charles, trying to remember what she was doing. As reality set in, she smiled and with an embarrassed chuckle lowered her head. "I am so sorry, this will do just fine. In fact, it's perfect."

Charles raised up and with a fake strained effort he helped her to her seat. Monica studied the table. She must have been looking around for a long time, because Charles had already laid out the delectable meal. Not one area of the table was vacant.

Charles removed one of the fine China plates that were tied with silk ribbon to the lid of the picnic basket. He filled it with smoked cheddar, summer sausage, and a slice of French bread. He then removed a crystal goblet from the basket and poured her a glass of Chardonnay. She accepted the meal and graciously set it down in front of her. It amused him that she was waiting for him to fill his plate before she would eat. She seemed so dainty.

"There is enough here to feed the whole town. Wouldn't you agree?" Monica asked.

Charles lifted one of the tiny morsels up, as if to examine it. Then he took a slow, deliberate bite, sinking his teeth into the cube size summer sausage. He held it in his mouth for a moment, savoring the taste. He peered up at Monica, noticing that she was also admiring him.

"I like to have an assortment, it stops one from becoming bored and it entertains the taste buds," he said in reply.

"Do you realize that we have not been properly introduced as of yet?" Monica asked.

Realizing that she was correct, Charles sat there as if pondering what to do with his chin resting in his fingers. Then standing up, he walked over to her and bowed. "May I present myself to you, dearest lady. I am former Sergeant Charles Hubbard and you are..." he said taking her hand in his and kissed the back of it tenderly.

"My dearest, sir, I am Monica Richardson and I am grateful for the lunch invitation," she sputtered out between giggles.

"It is not wise or polite to laugh in such a serious situation," he said with his lips jutted purposely out in a pout. Just seeing this scene made Monica start to laugh even harder, which brought a bright smile to Charles' face and soft ripples of laughter from him in return.

She realized, listening to his quiet laughter, that she was getting more and more attached to this stranger by the minute. His mannerisms were perfected, he was strong and agile. Even sitting here with him brought peace to her. She could tell just from the short time they'd been together that he was not a cruel man and never would be. *How could such a man exist?* She thought to herself. She didn't know or care, but here he was, serving her one of the best meals of her life.

"Why don't we eat now," he said as the laughter calmed down. Both ate in silence; they were both happy just to stare at each other. Finishing at the same time, Monica watched as Charles cleaned up the plates. When Charles reached over for her glass, their hands lightly touched for a moment. Monica looked up in surprise. They were face to face. She could feel the heat from his skin and his warm breath on her cheeks. As their eyes met, a warm sensation came over her. Monica just smiled and leaned away. Her skin gave off a pink glow, which Charles didn't ignore. He continued his chore with a gleam in his eye and a smile on his face.

Charles brushed the remains from the plate onto a small cloth and tied it with string. His beagle, Jonsey would love the leftovers. He decided to clean the plates later and just placed them back in the basket. With a mischievous grin spread across his face, he added more Chardonnay to her half-filled glass and handed it back to her.

"I thought it might be too early to drink. I didn't insult you, did I?"

"No, no insult at all. I just thought a perfect meal shared with a special lady, needs a toast," he said as he stood up. "To Ms. Richardson, may she grace my company many more times," he said leaning over and tapping the top of her cup with his.

She sipped the bitter liquid. It burned as it rolled down her throat. She was trying so hard to be the perfect lady, that she fumbled up and a drop of wine dripped from the corner of her mouth. Charles noticed this and very seriously reached over and dabbed the liquid away with his napkin. She felt his hands brush her cheek and right after that her palms began to sweat and her lips quivered. She looked up at Charles and her breath became still. She could see the raw emotions flicker from his impassioned eyes. It was the same emotion that racked her body.

He leaned forward, just slightly as to encourage a sweet reward. Monica knew what he wanted and became very nervous. No man had ever approached her with that notion in his mind. She felt a deep longing in her soul, but was not educated in such matters and had no idea about how to react. Her mind was frantically searching for the answer to her own question, *What to do?* The simple question was repeated over and over in her mind.

Charles saw the panic that crossed her face. He realized that she had never been kissed before. Charles prided himself on being a man of honor. So, he raised up his hand and pushed a stray curl away from her eyes.

"I will not do that again until you ask me, Okay?"

Relief flooded over her as she watched him return to his seat and the tiny lightening bolts that had jolted her body started to subside. It felt as if a warm blanket had come down and wrapped itself around her, holding her safely in it's folds. They stayed there a while talking and learning about each other for what seemed like hours. It wasn't until Charles mentioned the sunset that Monica actually realized how much time had passed.

"Charles, I am sorry, but it is time to retire for the evening."

He noticed that she was trying to rise and stepped around the table to assist her. She was glad to accept his assistance, after all she felt stiff from sitting for so long that her legs had fallen asleep.

"May I call on you again to join me for dinner?" Charles inquired.

"I would like that very much," she replied. "I stay at the Inn on Center Street when I'm in town. I am staying tonight and tomorrow night."

Charles was very pleased with that information, he would get to see her tomorrow also. He accompanied her to the Inn. After all that went on today, he still didn't want to leave her company. As they approached the multi-room house, Charles felt sad. The time went by to fast. Charles stopped just short of the porch and released her arm. "Till tomorrow my special lady." Then he turned and walked away whistling a merry tune.

Monica rushed into her rented room and went inside. As she turned to shut the door, she couldn't help but sneak one final look at his retreating back. Monica finished closing the door and leaned her forehead against the cold wood, closing her eyes. The warm feeling she felt earlier came back to her. It sent tingles all over her body, they traveled from the tip of her toes to the ends of her long auburn hair. This was all so new and wondrous to her. Monica mustered the strength to pull herself away from the door. As she prepared for bed, she thought about tomorrow, this was going to be a long night.

Chapter 6

Rubbing his eyes to remove the dry, crusty build up, Jeff forced his eyes open and wiped away the early morning tears that formed as he yawned. He stretched his arms out, feeling pain radiate up and down his back as his muscles strained in protest. The sunlight streamed into the room from the open curtains, forcing his foggy mind to realize that it was well into the day. Jeff pulled himself into a sitting position and rubbed his hands over his face, wiping away the last residue of sleep.

"What the hell…?" Jeff mumbled out loud as he picked up a piece of paper that slid off of his chest and onto the floor.

"Good morning sir." Jenny said from the doorway. "Did you sleep well?" The unexpected intrusion on his early morning quiet time actually perturbed him. He looked up at the doorway to see cook standing there. She looked so pitiful. Her blonde hair stood out in many different directions. Her cotton gown hung to the floor and was tattered and torn near the bottom where it dragged the floor. Deep, dark bags out lined her saddened brown eyes. His father had hired her because she was the best cook on this side of the county, but her appearance could use some help. He made a mental note to have Mrs. Thomas take her out for a new wardrobe. It would give him an excuse to get everyone out of the house so he could look around.

"I suppose I did. This davenport needs to be replaced. I want leather material, not this lame floral print, it was never my style. Why did you let me sleep here?" he asked between parched lips.

"Sir, I am so sorry. It's just that…well…you had such a traumatic day yesterday that when I brought dinner in you looked so peaceful, I…"

Jeff cut her off in mid-sentence. "Don't worry about it. Right now all I could really use is a cup of coffee."

"Yes, sir, I'll get some right away."

Jeff leaned back against the cushions that lined the davenport while listening to Jenny's retreating footsteps as she rushed out of the den to fetch the requested item. He felt awful, his eyes burned and he needed a bath. As he ran his fingers through his hair, a soft crackling noise caught his attention. He had forgotten the paper that lined his palm. Jeff carefully examined it.

The paper appeared to be very old. Yellow stains seemed to have spread over the entire face and the edges were lined in a dark brown color and appeared to have been torn. If this piece of parchment paper ever had straight edges, you wouldn't have known it.

The strange thing that puzzled Jeff was that it was in the shape of an upside down pyramid. Words had been printed on it and they were clearly written in bright red ink. It read: "My world has been turned upside down. I saw you push him and now your world will be dim." Sweat began to trickle down his face. Someone had seen him! But how? Jeff stood up and tossed the paper onto the end table. Jeff paced back and forth in front of the multiple bay windows. The forest green curtains gently swaying as he passed by them. He had come to full alert now, that note was most upsetting. *How could anyone know?* He asked himself. No one was home and the house was too far out of the way unless he had been followed. Jeff stopped and stood still for a few moments just glancing down at the floor.

Whoever wrote that note must be bluffing. He was sure of it. He had no enemies to speak of that would do anything this drastic. Just because he never had a prank pulled on him before doesn't mean it can't happen. Thought upon thought swirled in his mind. *What did this person mean?* Confusion and fear replaced his earlier thoughts of freedom from the monster to a new monster.

Jeff stomped over to the end table where his empty glass from last night was still sitting, glanced into the bottom of the cup then blew some dust out he saw there. Without even a second thought he stepped over to the bar, poured himself a stiff double of brandy and threw his head back as he drank it down in one gulp. He was in the process of finishing a second glass when Jenny appeared in the doorway with a fresh pot of coffee.

Jenny could not believe the sight in front of her. Just a few minutes ago he was a lifeless heap, barely moving. Now he was a nervous wreck who seemed to be drowning himself in liquor. She quickly covered her emotions and ignored him as she placed the trey on the serving table by the door. She brought some dry toast and cheeses along with a couple jars of jam to accompany the coffee. As she laid out the spread, she kept her back to Jeff, shuffling plates around pretending to be busy.

"Jenny?"

"Yes, sir," she said spinning around.

"Did we have any more visitors last night?" he asked setting down his empty glass.

"No, sir. Nobody came by."

"Are you sure?"

"Well almost sure. When I noticed that you were asleep. I cleaned up the kitchen and locked up the house, then went home."

"What about Mrs. Thomas? Is she awake yet?" he asked pointing toward the upstairs, as if to point to her room. He knew she would not do something like this and she had served his father and him since he was a child. She was a part of the family and as they were hers, so she lived upstairs.

"No, sir. Dr. Jeninson gave her that medicine to help her sleep, apparently, it worked wonders for her. Not one sound has come from her room all morning." Jenny stepped toward the door then turned to Jeff. "Do you wish that I should wake her?"

"No, Jenny, let her rest. Why don't you go and make the cream soup she likes? She'll have something to eat then when she comes to."

"That's a wonderful idea. I'll go and prepare it now."

Jeff walked over and sat back down on the davenport. Leaning forward, he rested his elbows on his knee and rested his head in his palms. The question plagued his mind again. How did they get in? That note did not have legs, someone had to have planted it. But who? And how? If all the doors were locked then the only way in would be windows! With that thought Jeff looked up and glanced from one window to the next in the room.

Standing up, he walked over to the closest window. Three windows lined this wall. The gardens could be viewed from this side of the house. He peered out, looking over the grounds. The vast gardens and an old workman's shed escaped his notice today. Evidence is what he searched for. The locks were all in place and the ground outside had not been disturbed. He received the same results from the other two windows. He looked at the end of the room to the larger bay windows that graced the room. Stepping around the corner desk, he reached out and pulled the heavy drapes back. Instead of opening from the bottom up like the previous three, these opened up from the side and swung outward. Again there was no sign of tampering anywhere. As before, he stepped over to the second set of bay windows and right as he reached for the drapes, it swayed away from him. His hand jerked back in response. Taking a deep breath, he yanked the drapes down from their holders. A loud cracking noise sounded as the brass bar crashed down to the ground.

The sound was so loud it startled even himself. His heart began to race and felt as if it was trying to break free from his chest. Taking a few moments to calm himself, Jeff took a few deep breaths in. Exhaling and inhaling deeply a couple of times finally had its calming effect. Jeff looked up and scanned the window. It was open a few inches and the glass had some how come away from the frame by the hinges. Looking outside Jeff could see his wood lines and again, no footprints, no dirt turned up, no sign of trespassing.

Jeff was looking outside when a hand reached out and grabbed his shoulder. Jeff's body jumped backwards and spun around. He hit the wall with his head and his elbow hit the window frame before he finally came to a stop on the carpeted floor.

"Ooh, Mr. Morris. Are you all right? I didn't mean to frighten you." Mrs. Thomas asked worriedly. A puzzled expression creased the aging lines of her motherly features. She had never seen him act like this before, so jumpy.

"I'm fine. You just startled me, that's all." Jeff stood up rubbed his injured elbow. "I was just lost in thought and Jenny said you were still in bed. But enough about me. Are you okay?" he inquired half-heartedly. He really had no interest in her feelings. Hell, he left the body for her to find.

"I think I'll be all right. It's just...well, I never had come across a body like that before," she said blinking back tears. "It was nerve racking, especially when it was someone you know and to see a sight like that." Her body started to shake as sobs racked her body again for the second time in two days.

"JENNY!" Jeff yelled down the hall.

"Yes, sir?" was heard followed by footsteps coming closer.

"Take her back to her room. Give her that sedative and make sure she gets some more rest. She's not well enough to be out of bed yet." Just as fast as the order was barked out, it was done.

Jeff took this opportunity to search the rest of the windows in the house. He prayed that no more surprises were in store for him, he doubted his heart could take another scare today.

Chapter 7

"Charles! Where have you been?" Congressman Sanders exclaimed and reached out his hand. "You have been gone, ooh, a year."

"Now, Jon, don't give me a hard time." A light smirk could be made out in his tone. "That beautiful young lady has kept my attention. It took me three days to get up enough will power to leave her side."

"You are not imposing on her honor are you?" Jon sternly interjected.

Holding his hands up, as if to defend himself. Charles backed up a few steps and laughed. "No, Jon. We became very close and talked for the last two days. She's so enchanting and beautiful. It takes all my strength to control myself. Have you ever had that problem?"

"Yes Charles I did. My late wife. I couldn't get enough of being around her. Just to sit next to her felt like a privilege." Jon Sanders sat back in his chair lost in the memory of his late wife. His mind screaming that he himself could not wait till they're together again.

"She seems to have a simple life, but at least she can take care of herself," Charles casually commented, bringing Jon back from his revelations.

"What does she do? And for that matter, who is she?"

"Well for starters her name is Monica Richardson and she inherited a saw mill down in Sandersonville. The town is only a couple of miles to the west."

"Yes, I know where that is." Jon interjected.

"Well, apparently her manager down there was scrapping some profits for himself. I went over her financial books with her and well…there was a huge amount of money missing. So I offered my services and now I'm the new manager of her mill," he said smiling.

"Well you finally have a job. That's good," Jon said as he turned and proceeded to turn toward the window. "Does this mean I won't be seeing you that often?"

"The town is only ten miles away. We will be able to get together on the weekends." Charles noticed the sad look that briefly swept over Jon's face momentarily. "I'm sorry if this upset's you. It's just that I plan to ask her to marry me."

Jon sat up in his chair and spun around. "Marry you?" he asked, surprised. You have only known her for a little more than three days. Isn't that rushing it a bit?"

"Jon, I fell in love with her the moment I laid my eyes on her. In addition, we developed a bond that is special and will last for all time." Charles sighed as the thought of Monica came to his love struck mind.

"What can I say? If she returns your feelings, then you have my blessings," he said smiling up at Charles. Deep down he thought it was a crazy idea, but once Charles has his mind set there was no changing it.

"Thanks Jon, I knew you would understand me. I just hope she says yes. Well, enough about my life. Have you received any news from the Governor about the lifting of the quarantine on the town?"

"If only I was that lucky," Jon said glancing down at the ground wearily. "The doctor in Boston is still searching for answers. He telegraphed me yesterday. He said that if it was Bubonic Plaque as the learned doctor from that damned University stated, then there's little if any chance of achieving our goal," he said, taking a deep breath in before continuing. "The only thing puzzling me is, the doctor in Boston stated that the plague has not made an appearance in many years. Plus, it was over seas and you have to have a rodent infestation along with unclean conditions."

"Jon, that does not make sense. You run a clean town and the most rodents I've seen are field mice that live around the feed stores."

"I thought about that. So I have sent a telegraph out to that learned doctor. I have not received a response as of yet. But I am not giving up hope," he stated slamming his fists down on the desk angrily. "I will get an answer if I have to send a notice every day. They will respond to me!" Jon sat there, staring at his enclosed fists. Waiting was the worst part. His career and all of his hopes depended on finding one man. Not forgetting to mention this town needs fresh money coming in. He had started the barter system just so poverty wouldn't ruin his people's lives. Some days he wished he had never been elected congressman. How can he do his job if he can't leave the town? The mayor doesn't seem to even be affected by all this. He just sits in his office down stairs, ignoring everything that crosses his desk.

"Charles, what about you? Do you have any connections out there?" Charles had thought about that very same question since he was informed that he couldn't leave.

"I don't have anyone or know anyone that could help. I've tried to think of whom I knew and no names came to mind. I am sorry. You know that I would help if I could." Charles looked away from Jon. That tiny lie held onto his tongue, leaving a bad taste. His uncle was the president's secretary and he could contact him. He didn't want to lie, it's just that ever since he met Monica, he didn't want to leave. It was ludicrous, he knew. He still had a promising future in the military and his families were well off, but it's just that he didn't want to leave her. Realization dawned on him. He had fallen in love. So, silently he hoped that Jon would not find his answers.

"That's too bad," he said rubbing his tired eyes. "So, you want to play some cards? Maybe getting our minds off of the problem will help for a while."

Charles happily agreed. Charles watched as Jon dealt the cards out for their game. In addition, he had time. He had another meeting in about two hours and had no plans on being late. His future depended on it.

Chapter 8

Charles guided Monica carefully up a steep set of stairs. A dark green cloth placed around her head, covering her eyes. It worked for his purposes for she couldn't even see light. Monica's mind was swirling with wonder. She could hear a wide assortment of sounds, but could not decipher any of it. Her palms had become very sweaty and were shaking. Where were they? What was going on?

All she knew was that Charles had left a list of instructions. The first thing listed was for her to wear her finest gown. So she picked out the canary yellow gown with the puffed shoulder cups and the v-shaped waistline. The second item was to pack a light lunch of just bread and wine. After completing Charles' second wish, she was just starting on the third, which was packing an over night bag with three days worth of clothes. Just as she shut the bag her front door flew open. High pitch voices and a whirlwind of color came rushing in and ran immediately over to Monica. A large woman with a boisterous voice approached her first. "Charles sent us to help you," one of the women excitedly shouted as a scurry of events began. One woman started brushing her hair, twisting in beads and formed light ringlets that hung down by her ears. Another closed up her overnight bag and carted it out the door. Two other petite women with long black hair opened a bag they had carried in, sat down and pulled out a variety of face paint and started applying it to her face. When all was done, she looked in the mirror. The face that stared back at hers was beautiful. She glanced around to make sure it wasn't someone else. The only time she had seen someone else with so much face paint was when she caught a glance at the women who worked at the saloons. The red lipstick and light pink blush along with tan eye paint made her think of one of the pictures she saw of the queens of England. She had never been pampered before and it felt strange, but wonderful all at the same time.

When the other women were content with their work, they ushered Monica out the door and into a carriage. Once she was seated an older women that was in the carriage handed Monica a letter and a blindfold. "Please put this on. Charles." Monica found this very strange but did as he asked. She brought the blindfold up to her eyes and tied it around her head. Monica's hands were sweating and her nerves were shaken. She had no clue as to where they were going or how long it would take, but she waited patiently, not asking any questions. It felt like an hour had gone by, but in reality it was more like twenty minutes, before the carriage finally came to a halt. As the door opened, Monica heard Charles' voice.

"My special lady, would you please accompany me inside?" Holding out his hand, he guided her out of her seat and down to the ground. Charles turned and guided her to a flight of steps. He paused a moment to look up at the two rows of robed men and women, who stood on either side of the steps. This group of people was his family, his belief and his heart. This was not his original coven, but they had accepted him with open arms. When he first came here, he noticed immediately that this was a one God fearing town. On Sundays he would just walk the streets of the town while everyone was in a church of one kind or another. As he rounded the corners of Main street and Franklin, he bumped into a rough sort of looking man.

They seemed complete opposites, but with an apology and a handshake they had become friends.

    Jim Flemming turned out to be one of the best friends that Charles ever had. Through him, Charles was introduced to this new coven and eventually had become a member. He still remembered the day he asked the High Priest for this wedding. It was like yesterday. After his card game with Congressman Sanders, Charles had walked the few streets to his High Priests and cautiously approached the subject closest to his heart.

    "You wish to have a traditional wedding Charles? Is that my understanding?"

    "Yes master," Charles replied without raising his eyes.

    The old man had a disbelieving smile on his face. He reached down and placed his hands on Charles' shoulder. Urging him to rise. "Charles you have been with the family for only two months. We were all leery when Jim brought you before us, but you did pass all the tests given to you. You could be a High Priest yourself," he said taking a few steps forward before stopping to look into Charles' eyes. "But do you understand what you are asking of us. The bride you have chosen is a Christian. She knows not of our ways. What makes you believe that she would agree to this?"

    "Master, Monica loves me and trusts me. She is a special women and I have told her of my ways. She didn't argue or throw me out. I know she will agree to this request."

    "Trust and beliefs are two different things, son. If she talks," the High Priest paused a moment to calm himself down, "we could all be in danger. People panic when they don't understand something and the old witch hunts could begin again. We have kept quite and stayed hidden, no one wants the old ways changed. All we ask…" he said straining to get his point across, "…is can WE trust her?"

    "I trust her with my life."

    "That's not enough, Charles. We require certain conditions, proof. I want you to be happy, but the protection of the coven comes first."

    Charles looked up and glanced into the aging, wise eyes. "I will blindfold her and lead her in that way. That should prove trust. Plus, if she talks, the coven may take the breath from my body." Charles stated soundly, while squaring his shoulders back and holding his head erect

The bright red robe that the High Priest wore, swayed around his bare legs as he stepped into an adjoining room. There he entered into a circle of some members that had congregated there. Reaching down, he pulled a doubled edged dagger from its sheath and motioned Charles to join him. Lifting the dagger into the air so that it was pointing up towards the sky, the High Priest announced Charles request to his coven.

"Charles has requested a traditional wedding! Do you grant this request?" As he asked each member present, Charles heart would skip a beat. His future depended on this night. Charles listened to each of their answers, hoping for more positive agreements than negative.

"Charles, please disrobe." Charles did as he was instructed. He was proud of his body and had no qualms about standing there with his entire splendor in plain sight.

"The coven votes 'aye'. Your wedding will be of the old ways. It shall be held on the night of the full moon, which is in two weeks."

Charles' features brightened as a smile came to his face. Excitement spread through him like a wild fire. The surge forced his manhood to stand out in the dim light of the room. The sound of whispering could be heard as a couple of the female members were over heard.

"Endowment is definitely not a short coming."

"Silence!" shouted the High Priest as he showed a disapproving look over the group. "This coven will close the pack, traditionally. The consummations between bodily pleasure and promises have been our way for many generations. It will be no different this time," he said stepping away. He will not participate till the end, as was also their way. "Charles, commence your pledge."

Charles nodded respectfully as he raised up his arms, holding them out and away from his defenseless body. Five women approached him and held each arm firmly while a third cradled his head. Together they lowered his body to the floor. Each person in turn spread Sandalwood oil over his entire body, saturating his skin with its enchanting smell. One women took the censor from the alter and made small circular motions over his body, allowing the sweet smelling smoke to settle around him before disappearing. Eight of the women stood up and joined hands, forming a circle around Charles' spread form. The men that had patiently sat by, finally rose up and slowly disrobed the circle of women, allowing them to lower themselves down to pleasure Charles' vulnerable flesh. Moans of pleasure slipped out of Charles' lips as numerous sensations bombarded him. It didn't take long for the rest of the group to follow suit of enjoying and consummating of the pledge with their physical sacrifices, until all were sated.

   Charles shook his head to clear his thoughts and took a few deep breaths in to calm down his excitement. That was then and this was now. He had upheld his promise, she was blindfolded and was willing. The wait would soon be over and he would bath in the paradise he knew awaited him.

Chapter 9

Jeff sat at his late father's desk with his head resting in the palms of his hands. Burying his father had been ten times easier and less tedious then trying to figure out these financial papers. It had taken damn near two weeks to gather all of the papers together. Between the lawyer and his fathers foreman Paul and the filing of the death certificate at City Hall, there ended up being thousands of ownership papers, receipts and business transaction forms as well as promissory notes. Well the only way to finish is to start one paper at a time.

So, first things first, he would have the lawyer wire all of the people named on the promissory notes their money. The last thing he wanted to be was indebted to someone he didn't even know. Second, he would telegraph Paul and inform him of his boss' demise and promote him to manager. Let him deal with the dirty railways. He didn't want any part of them. Next was the task of dealing with all of the receipts. Most were for tidily items, such as toiletries and hotel expenses. He would hand them over to the accountant for there was no reason for him to get worked up over them. The rest of the forms would take time to think over. They were all ownership papers. Jeff straightened the stack of forms and thumbed through them one at a time.

The first was *The River Lady*, a gambling steamboat. Next was Rochester, Inc., a clothing factory. On top of that there was The First Bank of Emerson. Emerson? Where was Emerson? Jeff was all but confused, most of the factory or businesses were in places he had never heard of. There were about fifteen more ownership receipts and none of them were duplicates. One shoe factory, one shipping firm, etc…

"I wonder if the lawyer knows about these," Jeff muttered out loud. If he didn't, he would have his hands filled trying to prove authenticity. After going over the papers, Jeff elected to search the other rooms that lined his father's hallway. Well, his hallway now. Jeff rose up and walked out of the master bedroom. Deciding to start with the closest rooms he started his dull task. The two rooms that were immediately on the left and right of the master suite were completely empty. They were even void of carpet and the dust that covered the floor was unmarred proving enough to him that no one had been in these rooms in decades. So, without disturbing one ounce of dust, he just left the rooms unscathed and locked the doors behind him.

On the left past the first door was a staircase that led upstairs, deciding to leave that area alone for now, Jeff proceeded to the door that was right after it. Entering that bedroom proved to be no adventure though, but it was strange nonetheless. The room was beautifully decorated, at least what could be seen through the cobwebs and dust build up. A fading rose-colored floral print lined the floors and wall trimmings. The center of the room was consumed by an overly large canopy bed. The two sides and the end of the bed were covered from ceiling to floor by sheer pink silk draper and it was dressed in rose patterned comforters and matching pillows with shams. Toward the end of the bed was a hope chest and on the right wall was a wardrobe closet. Watching his step as not to disturb too much of the dust on the floor, Jeff made his way over to the closet. Brushing the cobwebs away, Jeff swung the doors open and a light

I WILL HAVE YOU!

brown cloud of dust swirled around him, making him cough and gag until it finally settled. When he was able, he reached out and brushed away years of dust and decay from inside. A rainbow of colors met his eyes. Gowns of various designs and styles lined the rack. At one time the clothes were top of society, now they wouldn't do anyone any good.

Jeff stepped back and looked around the room. He wondered if his father had ever thought twice about this room. It was apparently decorated with love. The fine woods and intricate decorations were made to last a lifetime. Jeff paused a moment as realization hit him, this was supposed to have been his mother's room. It would have made her very happy, he was sure of that. Clean it up and redecorate it and this room would make a lady very pleased. Too bad it will stay empty. There was no family to fill these halls and there never would be.

Jeff finished searching the room to no avail, so he closed up the room and locked it for good. Directly across the hall was the last door in this hall, Jeff reached for the door handle to find it locked. How odd, why was this one locked? His father must have kept some of his private papers or past secrets in here, or so Jeff hoped. Jeff pulled out the key he used to lock the other doors and inserted it, nothing. The key didn't fit this lock, there were no other keys that could be found. So why is this one different?

Trying the key again, Jeff became angered at this turn of events. "Damn," he swore under his breath as he raised his leg and kicked in the door. Pieces of splintered wood shot out and sprinkled the floor with its debris as the door swung open. The force was so strong that the inside door handle embedded into the wall behind it, holding the door firmly in place.

Scanning over the room as he entered made the hairs on the back of his neck raise up. The walls were lined with sculptures and metal carvings of a horned beast surrounded by flame. The further he entered into the dark room, the more his nerves screamed at him to run. He held still for his curiosity got the better of him. Looking toward the north wall, Jeff could make out a table in the dim light. As he approached it to get a better look, he noticed it was covered in a black tablecloth that hung to the floor. On the top of the table were a set of matching gold candle holders in the shape of human skulls, two crystal globes were placed next to them and a rusted old dagger. Jeff lifted one of the crystal globes and brought it to eye level. The center of the globe was hollowed out and filled with a white powdery substance. Dipping his index finger into the bowl, he noticed it felt like sand and he noticed it had no smell so he brought it up to his mouth and tasted it: salt, it was salt. Shaking his head in wonder, he placed the bowl back down into its original spot. Jeff lifted the second globe and scraped his fingernail along the bottom. A light brown dried substance was visible under his fingernail, but he had no clue to what it was and he didn't want to try and taste it for fear it was blood.

Jeff backed away from the table, fear was replacing his curiosity. He would search this room later when there was more light. Then he would have everything in here burned. If he didn't fear losing his home he would do so now, it gave him goose bumps. Right now, he would just leave it alone and worry about it later, maybe provide a few tins of paint and new decorations and let Mrs. Thomas redo it. *Yes, that was a good idea*, he thought to himself as he back up toward the door. He couldn't help but take one more grim look at the room before rushing out, closing the broken door to the best of his ability. Jeff turned and sat down on the top step of the main stairwell, resting his elbows on his knees and his chin in his palm.

"Father. You were sick," he stated it as if his father was right there with him at that moment. Besides the search only proved how odd his father really was, but there were still no clues to that strange note.

"Who the hell is following me? And why?" Jeff shouted, determined to be heard this time. Jeff sat there for a while pondering all of the events and wondering where else he could look. He knew the house from the basement up, or so he thought, as he stared at the stairway leading up to the attic. He did need to search there, but he did not make one motion to move. After all these years, childhood fears still plagued him. Old nightmares of hidden bodies crept into his adult mind. Other memories of zombies attacking him the minute he put a foot on the first step. Memories of nightmares, that's all they were. Jeff tried to shake off the apprehensive feelings that racked his soul. He steeled his nerves, stood up and walked silently over to the stairwell.

Chapter 10

Congressman Sanders laid his head against the leather headrest of the tall back scarlet-colored chair that he had just ordered. He missed his old chair, but his office manager insisted on remodeling. The new cherry wood desk was now too short and his bookshelves were in total disarray. It was hard enough to find what he needed before, now it was impossible to even find a letterhead stationary. It would take weeks to get the office back in order.

Jon was sorting some papers on his desk when the office door opened and Benjamin Raley strolled in with a telegraph in his hands. "I was at the Post Office today and they asked me to deliver this," Ben said, handing the paper over. Jon glanced over the telegraph a moment and noticed it was dated for yesterday. It would be a miracle if anything was ever delivered on time. Jon ran his hand over his weathered features to try and hide the look of dissatisfaction from his life long friend.

Jon spun his chair around so it faced the window as Ben took a seat across from him. "Mr. Sanders. STOP. Studies still underway. STOP.

I WILL HAVE YOU!

Patients required. STOP. Will contact later. STOP. Dr. Jacob Levitz M.D. STOP."

Jon sat in stone cold silence for a few minutes. This was not the news he had wanted. The longer he waited the less time he had for the running. If he was going to further his career, he had to do something now, but what to do? If a solution doesn't present itself soon there would be no hope. Wading up the paper, Jon threw it toward the wastebasket. A low growl escaped from between his clenched teeth as the paper bounced off of the basket wall and landed on the floor. It seemed nothing could go right today.

"That bad, Huh?" Ben inquired looking down at the misbehaving paper ball. Jon glanced up at his friend. A worried look marred Ben's features. His normal God-like chiseled features were now crinkled up and gave the appearance of an aged man. The lines on his forehead resembled ocean waves and his eyes were drawn in.

Benjamin and he had grown up together. Each was the other's opposite. Ben was always calm while Jon's temper had a habit of flaring up because of the smallest problems. As Ben got older, he seemed to look younger, unlike Jon. Jon always appeared to be ten years older than what he actually was. It was very odd since they were the same age and shared the same birth date. Jon gave up years ago, he would always look older and that was because he led a more stressful life. As Jon sought out a political position, Ben had become a lawyer. Both had esteemed jobs, but Jon thought Ben's was cushiony. While Jon was in City Hall and always busy, Ben had set up his practice on Main St. Ben was lucky in one aspect, he was the only lawyer in the surrounding area. He represented just about everyone, including Jon.

"Not necessarily bad news, Ben, just no news. My future is at a dead end and there are no openings in sight," Jon spit out while running his chubby fingers through his short black hair. An exasperated breath of air sounded out as Jon loosened his collar and tie. The air seemed so stuffy and with the stress on top of it, droplets of sweat will be his best friend for the remainder of the day.

"Ben, if I can't get the people of South Carolina on my side I'll never get the Governorship. How can I get the position if I can't travel around? The people need to hear my words and become acquainted with my face."

Ben paused to think about his friend's dilemma. He wanted to offer some kind of encouragement, but what could be done? What to say? Ben reached down and lifted up the wayward ball and placed it into the trash receptacle, then sat up and laced his fingers together behind the back of his head.

"It was so much simpler five years ago. We could come and go as we pleased. We were reliant on no one. People would travel through and spend their money and we would gladly wave goodbye as they left. Now the state has to leave livestock for us to pick up or goods for that matter. That damn ruling five years ago only brought agony to this town," Ben stated.

"True, Ben, so true. Our people are now starving because of this war. The livestock and goods have not been delivered in two months. The governor has to lift the quarantine."

"Who says the governor has to lift it? Have you tried going over his head? Look," Ben sputtered out as if racking his brain, "the person that gave the ruling for the quarantine was not a doctor, correct?"

"That's right. It was a medical student. The University in Boston claimed to be too busy to have an M.D. look into "some small town's problems," so they gave us a student."

"That is perfect. What we're going to do is go over the Governor's head. I'll appeal to the Supreme Court. We will put a lawsuit against the University. That will force all of the medical and legal dealings in to the public eye. Once all the forms are filled, I'll petition the courts to do an investigation into this matter. They will have no choice but to comply. The law is the law after all."

Jon stared at Ben for a while before a broad grin graced his face. When Ben smiled that meant hope was in the air. Just knowing that hope existed again, numerous thoughts jumped around in Jon's head, all he needed was a time line.

"How long do you think this would take?" Jon inquired.

"I would think about six months."

"Six months? That long?"

"Jon, you have to look at it this way. There is a war going on that we have to work around. Other than that, it would usually have only taken three months. I'm adding in for extra time. It could actually be shorter." Ben said sitting upright by now, resting his entwined hands on the desk in front of him.

"What do we need to do to get this started?" Jon eagerly asked. He was getting more and more excited over the option of breaking free from a dead end road.

"First Jon, what you need to do is to call a town meeting. Have everyone attend. I will give all of the detail of what we're hoping to accomplish then. Plus, I know this is an old tune, but money is not an option. We will need plenty of it. I don't care how it gets raised. Just remember, without it, we go no where."

"Okay. That's no problem. When do you think you will be ready for us to hold a meeting?" Ben reached over the desk and removed a blank piece of paper and grabbed Jon's pen out of his breast pocket. He jotted down a few notes before finally looking up at Jon.

"Give me two days. I will have everything figured out. I will need a medical affidavit from Dr. Jeninson. Having inside medical opinions will greatly enhance the turn over."

Jon leaned back in his chair, this was getting better and better. If Ben could pull this off, they could be home free. All that was needed now was planning. He would do everything needed of him to gain their freedom from this cursed town.

"Ben, I'll go talk to Doc myself. If he has kept any information, you will have it in the morning. I guarantee it," Jon vowed as he stood up. "One question though, how is this going to speed up the process? I only ask because I need some clarification for the people."

Also standing, Ben turned to face Jon. "Once a suit is installed against the school, the courts will pull all of the records and then study the medical evidence."

"Why do you think they would even consider our case?"

"You have to look at it from the Governor's point of view. Once he receives the papers from the courts, he can no longer ignore us. I can contact everyone via telegraph and ask for a ruling on this matter. I don't need to be there as long as I have communication," Ben stated, beaming a bright smile at Jon.

"That is brilliant! Start the ball rolling and I'll be sure that no slack comes loose. The last thing we want is a screw up this that late in the game."

Sensing the meeting was over, Ben stepped over to the door. Turning to Jon once again Ben extended his hand out to his jaunty friend.

"I hope this works," Jon tenderly added.

"I believe it will. I'll go right now to Judge Benson's and get the order processed. It should only take a few minutes. He should be elated by the news."

"Well hurry now," Jon said, taking the hand offered, "daylight is fading."

With that Ben stepped out of the room and Jon returned to his desk to reflect on their conversation. As he sat down and laid his head back a smile again broadened his chubby, wrinkled features. With this new revelation, he wiggled excitedly in his seat. His future was looking up. Taking a piece of stationary out, he started a list of all of the things he would need.

Chapter 11

Monica jumped as a loud thud echoed through the hall as the front doors were closed behind her. The sound so eerie, that goose bumps formed on her arms. "Where are we?" she carefully asked. Charles heard the fear creep into her voice and knew that if she did one thing wrong he would pay with his life. Lowering his head until it was next to hers, Charles squeezed her hand and whispered in her ear.

"Do you trust me?" he asked.

"Yes I do, but this isn't like you. What's going on?" she asked squeezing his hand in return.

"Shh, be patient. You will find out very soon." With that said, he brushed the back of his hand against her quivering cheek before leading her forward. Monica followed silently behind Charles. She would wait just because he asked her too, but it didn't make the chills go away that had come over her.

As they walked further into the room, Monica noticed the hard floor they were once on, was gone. Somehow, it now felt cushiony. Charles bent down and coaxed her to join him. She expected to feel the cold, hard ground beneath the hand she lowered to steady herself, but instead was welcomed by the softest fur she had ever encountered. By this time, her legs had become very wobbly. The thought of sitting down was most appealing, so she followed without incident. Many different sounds and voices, as well as the rustling of clothes could be made out in Monica's limited senses. She did detect a hint of jasmine in the air. It helped to calm her nerves and she sat and waited. Monica was momentarily startled as Charles cupped her chin in his hand. She nuzzled it like a kitten, letting the prickly, warm sensations that this small amount of contact brought, spread across her skin.

"Do you wish to marry me?" Charles asked hoping he was not wrong. Monica smiled and went to remove the blindfold. Charles quickly grabbed her hands, halting their movements. "Do not remove it, please. It must stay on, for if you peek, the magic will go away." Charles inhaled a deep breath. Hearing the serious tone in Charles voice, Monica lowered her hands and listened as Charles continued. "You know my beliefs are not of the Christian way. Accepting me for your lifetime partner and mate also means accepting all that I am. Can you blindly enter into my world with perfect love and perfect trust?"

She knew he was not Christian, but she had not inquired about it. All she concerned herself with was the acceptance that could withstand all differences and she could. "Yes I can. I have never doubted you and I will trust you now. Yes I will marry you. I love you with all my heart."

Pride and love washed over him like a tidal wave. He could not believe his luck. She could not be the perfect woman. One just did not exist in this entire world. If there was a perfect woman though, it would be she.

Monica reluctantly released Charles hand as she felt him pull away. "Just wait here and no matter what you hear or feel, please do not try to remove the blindfold. All right?"

"All right, Charles," she answered. All she could do was wonder and wait as she heard his footsteps retreat away from her.

Charles had only taken a few steps away from her before he turned and approached the High Priest. Charles bowed his head and kneeled down in respect. The long black robe that he wore, surrounded his whole body, engulfing him in the folds and then crumpled around his feet as it touched the floor. The hood of the cape draped just far enough down over his eyes that is concealed his thoughts in front of the High Priest.

A few moments passed in revered silence as the High Priest stood watch over the group that had assembled. He looked out of place in his bright red robe, while the other's were adorned in all black, including the High Priestess, but unlike the others robes, hers was adorned with gold trimming. The difference was definitely noticeable among the group.

Charles impatience forced his eyes to peer up, wandering what was taking so long. Just as he did so, the High Priest raise up his arm and placed it on top of Charles' head and held out his other hand to summon the Priestess. As the Priestess came forward, she removed a crystal bowl from the altar. Charles watched as she approached him and knelt down by his side. Using her index finger, she lifted his hardened chin up, forcing him to face her.

Charles watched as she dipped her fingers into the bowl and brought them up to his face. A cold, wet, and beautiful smelling liquid dripped down his face as the Priestess drew a star and then circled it for protection on his forehead. Then she sprinkled the sweet-smelling liquid over his cloaked body.

"Will she protect this coven and not shame us or betray us?" she said looking deep into Charles' blue eyes.

Without hesitation, Charles quickly answered back. "I know she will. She has a good heart and she knows of my ways and accepts them."

"Would you give your life for this coven and her?" she carefully inquired.

"I have already sworn with my last breath to do so and I will uphold to my word."

Hearing the questions thrown at Charles made her palms sweat and she started to shake. What did this all mean? Was he willing to give up his life for her? Her nerves became instantly alert. What are they going to do to him? As much as she wanted to look, she kept her word also. She would just wait. Monica twitched a little when she heard footsteps approaching her and felt the cushion of fur compress as this unknown person seated themselves next to her.

"My dear Monica, is your love as true as his? Does your heart race just to hear his voice?" A few quiet moments passed. "Tell us now, child." The words came out like a whisper on the wind. Everyone that was present became instantly quiet. They all listened carefully and became alert to her every word.

"My love can burn brighter than any candle. It can and will traverse the highest mountain if it was required. It could overcome death and all forms. Charles has become my reason for living. I have come to know him and know he is of good intentions. I could not have trusted him thus far if I did not love him."

Upon hearing her words the High Priestess again repeated her actions of placing a star on her forehead along with a circle. The blindfold absorbed any liquid that would have dripped down across her face, turning the wet area into a dark green patch. Then she stood up and walked back over to the High Priest's side.

Monica was kept in the dark as to the reason for the up and down and round motions on her skin, but the cold liquid did send shivers up her spine. One thing she did know is if this is to be the way, then so be it. No harm was to come to her, Charles promised.

The High Priest, satisfied with the answers, proceeded with the ceremony. "By the powers of Earth, Air, Fire, and Water, I decree that both who give willingly of themselves to the other's soul are now joined as soul mates in this world and the next for all eternity. Blessed be."

A giant roar sounded from the group and echoed throughout the great hall as the celebration began. Charles stood and walked back over to Monica and kneeled down beside her. "Trust me," he whispered in her ear. "Don't fear me, just let yourself feel."

Charles held onto Monica's hand as he raised up and looked at the group that attended his blessed day. "I have known this woman in many ways except one. She has not feasted on the flesh of a man. I have sworn my life to her and in this I offer my body as well." With that said, Charles raised up Monica's hand and placed it on his chest.

Monica could feel the throbbing of his heart and felt the heat from his naked chest. It was a little unnerving to feel bare skin. The knowledge that he was without a shirt in front of all the people in the room, sent small chills over her body. She instinctively reached up, searching for his face. Charles laced his fingers through hers, bringing her hand up to his cheek. She started tracing her fingers over his strong jaw line before tracing his lips. Charles opened his mouth and gave her finger a small nibble.

Shivers of pleasure raced though Charles' body. She had never taken the liberty of studying his body in this fashion before, it was wonderful. Charles looked behind Monica and nodded his head at the crowd behind them, telling them it was time to start.

Monica jumped when she felt hands on her back, they seemed to be unbuttoning her dress. It was so strange as she was urged to turn this way and that as all of her clothing was removed from her body by multiple sets of hands. In her shyness, she crossed her arms over her chest.

"Trust in me, my love," Charles said reaching out to her hands and gently pulled them down to her sides. "Do not be ashamed in your flesh. It is so natural and beautiful to behold. Please don't hide it from your husband."

On hearing Charles' calming voice, Monica squeezed her fingers into a fist, but left them at her sides as the last remnants of clothing were removed from her body. Tiny droplets of sweat had appeared on her body, making it glisten in the candlelight.

Charles watched as the coven members finished undressing her. He decided to keep the secret from her that men and women alike had undressed her. A virgin being undressed by numerous people could become unnerving and the last thing he wanted her to be was a timid wife. The sharing of the body was a blessed celebration of life and he would be the first to have her.

Charles approached Monica very steadily. Reaching out, he ran his hands down her silky arms. Then guided her down to the fur blanket beneath them. "Move only to touch, not to pull away," he whispered into her ear before applying light kisses to her lobes, then slowly began caressing her body.

She did as he asked. The more his hands caressed her body the harder it was to restrain herself from pushing him away. The sensations that spread over her were so new to her and just a little frightening. She soon became light headed and a heat slowly crept up her thighs, making her yearn for more.

Charles leaned over her and swept her lips with his, then traced the outline of her mouth with his tongue. She raised her head up to meet his lips, just as she felt his skin, he backed away.

"No yet, my love," he said. Tingles spread through her breasts as the tip of his tongue circled their erect peaks. Her soft flesh was begging to be caressed. A warm trail was left by him as he worked his way down her flat tummy.

Monica stiffened momentarily as he raised her leg and placed it onto his shoulder, forcing her legs to open for him. He had to remember to pace himself and slow down. The excitement surging through him was about to explode. If that happened, the moment would be lost.

Wondrous sensations careened through her body as the warmth and moisture from his mouth met her soft folds. He had waited so long to taste the sweet nectar that she kept hidden that he rapidly consumed her, bringing her to the brink of oblivion within moments. Wave after wave of ecstasy crashed over her body. Moans of pleasure echoed through the hall and vibrated through the onlookers. Again Charles started to lap at the succulent juices, he just couldn't get enough of the sweet ambrosia that was flowing from her.

And as before a heat built up inside of her, so hot, so strong that she thought it would surely burn her. It grew higher and stronger. She tried closing her legs, but they would not obey her commands. Lights appeared in her eyes, like a million stars exploding at once.

Charles released her as a scream rang out from her lovely lips. He watched as the sweet tasting liquid streamed out of her body. He swirled his finger around her opening, lifting the cream of life from it's hidden cave and traced her lips with it.

Monica ran her tongue over her moistened lips, tasting the liquid. It was sweet to her pallet and very arousing that she reached out in a fury, bringing his hand closer to her open mouth. Running her tongue up and down his drenched finger, she sensually cleaned his finger of all remnants.

Seeing her in such a frenzy made Charles want to join her. Raising her legs until her knees touched her breast. Charles raised up and positioned himself before sliding into her moist folds. He was met with a small amount of resistance, as she was unknown to man. He plunged forward inside of her in one swift motion. The welcoming heat sent shivers racing down his back. He relaxed a moment when he felt her body jerk and heard her let out a small cry as her virginal membranes were ripped away. Charles leaned over and kissed her cheek, then her eyes, before overtaking her lips. He felt her responding again, so he slowly pushed into her and withdrew. As she started to match his rhythm, pace for pace, his control threatened to break loose. He quickened and hardened his pace. He would withdraw just to slam back into her receptive body. Her breathing had started to escalate in force as she would rise up and meet his thrusts. Sweat had built up on Charles skin from the strain he was using to hold himself back. Just as he thought he couldn't hold back anymore, Monica's body raised up against him, lifting him off of the floor. As she came up, he wrapped both his arms around her back and held on while they both met their release. The ecstasy filled screams that accompanied their release was animalistic in sound.

As their pulse slowly returned to normal, Charles looked around the room in wonder as multiple sets of eyes stared in amazement. The true passion that flared from both of them was raw and unhindered, the likes of which they have never known.

Chapter 12

Benjamin Raley stood outside of the Post Office, which doubled as the towns telegraph office and stared at the yellow sheet of paper in his hands. A grin spread from ear to ear as he read the broken words.
"Mr. Raley. STOP. Received your papers. STOP. Supreme Justice Shelton is looking into matter. STOP. Please send doctors' report. STOP. Will notify upon evaluation. STOP. Supreme Court Secretary M. Johnson. STOP."
"Good morning, sir." A gentle voice greeted Ben bringing him back to the present.
"Good morning to you also ma'am," he parried as he removed his hat and side stepped to allow the lady to pass. "Good day, ma'am." He politely remarked as the woman continued on her way.
A doctor's report, that's right. Jon said he would get it for him and never did. Ben stood there on the old dusty wood planks that the town called their side walks and pondered what was the next move. The town had held their meeting two nights ago and it was a unanimous decision to file with the courts. The whole town also was nice enough to pledge money for the cause. There was nothing

standing in his way except the Congressman. He was more occupied with his future than what it takes to get it. Right then and there Ben decided to go to Dr. Jeninson's office and get the papers, after all, he was the lawyer handling the matter.

Dr. Jeninson was in his office filling away patient folders, this was a normal routine, since he didn't have room or the money to pay an assistant. Being it was almost closing time and all of his patients had gone home, he opened the top drawer of his desk and took out his bottle of whiskey and a glass. Just as he was pouring the first glass, the bell over his door sounded as the door opened.

"Ben, what are you doing here?" he said quickly putting away the glass and bottle.

"I needed the papers from the sickness. Jon was supposed to pick them up, but he never delivered them. Do you still have them?" Ben inquired as he pulled out the only chair for visitors.

"I do have them. Jon did come in, but I told him that it would take a few days to get all of the information together. Would you like to have the entire report?" Dr. Jeninson turned around to his small filling cabinet and opened the door and pulled out the first folder. He knew right where it was. He didn't want to chance misplacing this important information. His future depended on all of the events to come also. He always dreamed of a practice with four to five rooms and an assistant to do all of the paper work. It was his dream to have much more than what he has now. Right now, he was working with the barter system. Patients would bring him food or do his laundry and that worked for now, but he wanted more.

"Here you go. I haven't made copies so don't loose them," he said handing the thin folder over. Ben opened the folder to find only three sheets of paper inside. The first page described the symptoms and visible marks on the sick. The next page outlined the number dead and how long it took from the time the first signs of the sickness 'til the death. The final page explained the disposal of the bodies and how long the fires burned. It wasn't much information in his eyes.

"Shouldn't this be say…thicker? Is this enough information for the courts?"

"The courts will not require a patient by patient report, since they all had the same sickness and the time lines were all the same, as was disposal. The courts don't like having to go over a thousand page report for something as repetitive as this disease seemed to be. If an educated doctor reads the report, he will be able to define its material. I know the courts will get the best doctor's to look over the case, since a Governor is covering up something like this."

Ben closed the folder and set it down on the desk. "Mark, let me ask you something. In your professional opinion, do you think we have a chance?"

Mark looked up at Ben. He looked so worn out and this matter was just starting. He knew Ben needed reassurance, it could be a short road or it could be a long rough road. It was definitely going to take its toll on Ben's nerves. "Yes I do. Why wouldn't we? I believe we just had a severe case of small pox. That disease is not a reason to quarantine the town for this long of time."

Ben was satisfied with that answer. He had thought the same, but being he was a lawyer and not a doctor, it made a big difference if he said it or a professional did. "Thank you Mark. I'll take these over and send them over the telegraph. I know it will cost more than mailing it, but it will be faster. When I'm done, I'll bring them back and you can make copies. The courts will still need the original report sent to them."

Mark stood and accompanied Ben to the door. "Good luck Ben and I'll see you tomorrow." With that Ben left and Mark resumed his plans. Sitting back down, he removed his glass and bottle and poured himself a double. "God, I hope this works. We all need a prayer." And with that, he gulped down the first of many drinks.

Chapter 13

"Sir, is there anything else you need?" Mrs. Morris asked as she cleared the dinner table.

"No, thank you," Jeff replied as he pushed himself away from the table, leaving his still full plate sitting there. He had no appetite of late. Ever since he found that room upstairs, he had been haunted. Fear kept him so much at bay that he had not even told the staff about what was up there and had no idea when he would.

Standing up and excusing himself to his den, Jeff relaxed with a glass of brandy, as was his routine every night. He sat there pondering the riddle of the notes. By now he had received three of them. Unlike the first one, these only had one word on each of them. The first, he found the day after his father's death. The next two were found three days ago. One was placed on his bed. It was of the same yellowed paper and written in red ink was the word "sad." He found the third note in his carriage as he went to make his morning rounds two days ago. Again, it was on yellowed paper with red ink and the word "family" written on it. Jeff was even more confused. None of this was making any sense and he still didn't have a clue as to who was planting them.

Laying his head back, he thought about the last few days. He chose to continue his search and went up the stairs that led to the attic. Unfortunately, all he found was disappointment. For such a feared room, it proved to be no big deal. Dusty floors and cob web covered windows. The only thing that stood out was one chest sitting in the middle of the room. It had been left without a lock and what was left of the leather straps that wrapped around it were laying on the floor. Age had taken its toll on this once beautiful brown chest. It reminded him of an old pirate chest. It took some force to open the lid. The rusted hinges did not want to give up their secret easily. Jeff pushed with all his might, lifting up the front of the chest back. Then "thump," the chest lid opened and the bottom of it crashed back down onto the floor.

Cautiously, not to disturb any rodents that may have been in there, he reached in and lifted out some clothe material and lifted it out. Jeff shook the dust off of the blue material, just to find it was a man's shirt. He set it down and pulled one piece of clothing after another out of the chest. Jeff had no interest in what type or color they were as he threw them down, one by one, onto the floor. When he finally reached the bottom of the chest, hope sprang up inside of him. There in the bottom was a small green box the size of a cigar box.

Jeff lifted it out and opened it up. Inside the box was a picture of a man and a women holding each other, they looked very much in love. The women very much resembled his mother, but healthier looking. He had no clue as to the identity of the man, he was very rugged and westerly type, with his wide brimmed hat and much used leather chaps. He look very happy and very much in love. Who was he? And what does this have to do with his life. It was definitely his mother, but why was she holding on to this man. As he went to place the lid back on the box, he heard something sliding around. He removed the picture and there in the bottom was an old key and a map. Jeff lifted up the key and swirled it back and forth as he looked it over, then placed it in his pocket as he picked up the map. He knew the area the map depicted, some of the streets are now named, but the general outline is downtown. The only item out of place was an "X" that was marking the alleyway off of Bently St. Just four blocks from Main St. He would have to visit this area, Jeff made a mental note as he walked back down the stairs, leaving the clothes and the chest in disarray.

Chapter 14

Charles and Monica had fallen instantly into a comfortable schedule in the last three months. They had agreed to live in Monica's parents' home. It was closer to the saw mill where Charles went to work everyday and it had more room. Life had finally attained a perfect sense of worth. Charles would go to work and near the end of the day, Monica would do mending and the cooking, then would be waiting for him at the door when he arrived home.

Today would be different though. Monica watched as Charles went off to work, just as soon as he was out of sight, she dawned her winter garb and waited for the carriage to arrive that she had ordered yesterday. It couldn't get there quick enough for her own liking. She had a plan and hoped she could achieve it before Charles came home. Unlike the other days, where she would stay home and do chores, today she was going shopping.

When the carriage finally arrived, she could hardly contain her excitement. She snatched her winter coat from off the davenport and flew out the door. She didn't leave a note because it would ruin the surprise and she planned on being back before Charles came home.

She sat and stared out the window of the carriage as it rumbled down the muddy, pot-marked road. Christmas was around the corner and time was passing by very quickly. A chill was in the air and the wind that blew in through the carriage window was so crisp it bit at her tender skin. The snow always came late and never lasted very long, but while it was here, it was beautiful. The bare trees were laden with natures white crystals and the ground sparkled like a million diamonds gleaming under bright light. The sight of freshly fallen snow was so entrancing that Monica just watched as it floated to the ground. The white flakes ranged in different sizes, from small ones the size of peas to large ones the size of walnuts. She just wanted to reach out and catch one, but the carriage was speeding along and she doubted that even one of them would stick to her gloved hand without getting blown away.

"We're almost there, ma'am. It's 438 Center St. Correct?"

Hearing the driver calling out to her made her realize that the town was approaching. "Yes driver, that's correct."

It only took a few moments more for them to reach their destination. The driver reined in the horses and the carriage rattled to a halt. Monica waited while the driver climbed down and came to open the door. She accepted the out stretched hand and used her other hand to lift her skirts just above her ankles, as not to trip. The hard packed snow creaked in protest as her booted foot touched down upon it.

"What time does the carriage make it's return trip?" she inquired.

"Two o'clock and we don't wait," he rudely commented.

Monica could not believe the rudeness in his voice, so turning away she sharply replied, "Then I should hope not to be late." And turned her back abruptly and walked away.

Monica paused on the street corner across from her destination. In bold letters were the numbers 438. Looking up at the street sign confirmed she was where she was suppose to be, "Center St.", Congressman Sanders home. Taking her Christmas list out of her pocket, she glanced over it for the first time since she wrote it.

"Let's see," she murmured to herself, "some quilting material for Suzanne, yarn and saddle soap for Jim and Nancy, and of course a ledger for Mr. Sanders."

Normally she wouldn't get a gift for someone she hardly new, but Mr. Sanders was the exception. Being a Congressman, he had thrown a beautiful and elaborate Thanksgiving party that Charles and she had been invited to. While there, Charles had kept eyeing a certain rapier. Mr. Sanders had informed them that it had belonged to Captain John Sawyer, a pirate. About sixty years ago, the man was known as the pirate of the pacific. He was credited with the sinking of *The Mirage*, a frigate. It was rumored that the son and the wife of the King of England were aboard, but the only confirmation came from stories passed down from one drunken mariner to another.

Whether the stories were true or not did not matter to Monica. The way Charles looked at it made no difference to her of it's authenticity. So, later that evening she had approached Mr. Sanders about purchasing the precious item. To her surprise, he not only agreed to part with it, but he was giving it to her and the only stipulation was to take care of it, which she quickly agreed to do. They made arrangements for her to pick it up at a later date and that date was today, but after looking over her list, she decided to change her plans slightly. Between the swords length and weight it would be to difficult to lug it around to do her shopping, plus in her estimation it would be just down right rude of her to show up without a gift after the kindly gesture that was being shown to her. She would finish the rest of her shopping then return.

Looking up the street, Monica decided to start at the General Store then work her way back here, so she turned and walked the block over to Main St. As she approached the corner, the jingle and rattle of a carriage approaching caught her ear. She stopped on the edge of the sidewalk and waited for the carriage to pass. She didn't have long to wait though. A solid black horse raced past her followed by a brown wagon that was sliding side to side on the icy road. As the driver tried to take the corner at a speedy pace, the poor animal lost it's footing and slid to the ground pulling the wagon onto it's side with it.

I WILL HAVE YOU!

A lump formed in her throat as the distorted and now broken wagon careened out of control and started sliding towards her. Monica took a few steps backwards as the wagon bumped up onto the curb, startling her even more. Not worrying about anything else except to get away, she turned to run, but the heel of her boot hooked on an old brick that stuck out of the sidewalk and she fell backwards towards the hard ground. Trying to stop her fall, she put her arms back to try and catch herself. Just as she met the ground a fierce pain shot up her left arm.

Instinctively, she raised up the injured arm. In doing so, the movement forced her head to fall back to the bricked ground. Through her blurred vision and pain she tried rising up just to be over taken by dizziness. Just as a deep darkness started to settle in around her, a shadowy figure of a man loomed above her. That's all she could see before she passed out.

Chapter 15

    Jeff Morris was making his morning rounds. Same old dull drums. He would go to the bank and make his daily deposits. Since his father's death his bank bag had been hefty, even for this town. Then he would go to the General Store and sit and watch the men play chess. It had become a normal routine and he kind of liked it. He had always been a hermit, but this newfound life appealed to him immensely.
    Jeff had just rounded the corner of Main St. and Center when he was bumped in the leg by something very heavy. Looking back over his shoulder, it became very clear that it was a run away wagon. As he turned to cross the street, the sight of a person collapsing caught his eye. Jeff raced over to the figure that lay motionless on the ground. Seeing that the wagon was still not under control, he lifted the frail figure into his arms and carried her into the Post Office. As he laid her down on the counter, he yelled out for someone to fetch the doctor.
    Nobody seemed to move right then and there, so Jeff reached over the counter and grabbed the first thing that he could reach. The next thing anyone knew, a wooden stamper went flying across the room

toward the small crowd that had appeared.

"Look, there are four people in this room. One is unconscious and another one is holding her. Now if the two other people are not doing anything worthwhile, I suggest you go and get the doctor." Jeff smirked at the two attendants. His eyes were so full of rage that both men ran out the door without looking back.

Careful not to disturb her, Jeff removed his arm from behind her neck and her knees. With his hands free he removed his coat and balled it up and gently placed it under her head. After making sure she was as comfortable as possible he brushed some stray strands of hair away from her chilled face. He knew it would take time to fetch the doctor, so he decided to take advantage of the time and make sure she was fine. He lowered his face till it almost touched her lips to check her breathing. As he did so, he couldn't ignore the picture of beauty presented to him. Jeff took the back of his hand and caressed Monica's cheek, feeling the warmth return to her skin. He trailed his hand down over her lips, across her chin to her throat. Feeling a strong pulse, he traced the outline of her collarbone. Such beauty. Where did this angel come from? Even though he was not a doctor, he found the examination of this wounded women very stimulating. As his eyes looked her up and down, he was held entranced. As he watched her, a small red droplet landed on the counter top.

Seeing blood, Jeff snapped to. He lifted one arm then the other before he found what he was looking for. The white fur surrounding her left wrist was soaked through. Being extra careful now, he slipped the coat sleeve off of her arm and slowly traced his hand down her arm and lifted her hand up just enough to slide his palm under hers. He was still holding her hand when the sound of horses hooves drew near. Jeff looked up as the doctor rushed in the room. Bending down, Jeff placed a gentle kiss on the back of her hand before anyone could see. Upon doing so he saw the wedding band for the first time. His face crinkled up into menacing lines. This was not a good thing. Married, she was married. Remembering the doctor was present Jeff cleared the look from his face and spun around. He would deal with this matter later.

"Doctor Jeninson," Jeff said offering his hand.

"Jeff," the doctor countered and took the hand offered. "What do we have here?"

Bending over Monica, Dr. Jeninson started to remove her coat. Jeff ogled the sight. The first thoughts he had when he first spied her were of ungentlemanly nature. Even still the thoughts lurked in his mind. So, he started to assist the doctor in disrobing his patient.

"It's a young lady that had fallen. A horse had gone crazy and I don't know if the wagon it was hauling hit her or not," he said as he started to peel the top part of her dress down and away from her neck. Right before it reached her breasts the doctor held his hand up to stop Jeff.

"That's far enough, Jeff. She still needs to keep her dignity. I would hate for her to wake up and have two men standing over her half naked body," Doc commented with a grin and a sly wink. Being careful not to injure her any further, he started his examination. Starting at the top of her head, he lifted her eyelids to view her pupils, then turned her head side to side in smooth motions and listened for any unusual sounds. Instead of sounds his hands came in contact with a warm, sticky liquid. He turned her head just a little further to the side and there was the wet culprit. Blood splatter was present on the makeshift pillow and the counter right below her head and neck. There wasn't a lot thankfully, but her hair had left tiny scratch marks in the drying blood.

"She has a head injury. We'll have to clean the area. I'll need some hot water and pillow ticking. It will need bandaging immediately," he said without looking up.

"Doc, there is blood on her arm also. I noticed it while we were waiting," Jeff said and pointed out the bloodstained sleeve. Doctor Jeninson lifted Monica's wrist and tore back the sleeve of her gown. The arm was severely disfigured. The bent v-shape that the bone had formed was not going to be easy to set.

"Jeff, I need you to hold her arm around the elbow. We are going to reset her arm." Glancing over his shoulder he noticed the multiple bystanders, "You," he said pointing at a young boy, "go and get me two straight sticks, Hurry. And you," he said, picking the postman out of the crowd, "find me some twine and make sure it is at least two feet long."

It didn't take long for the requested items to arrive. "Are you ready? Hold tight and don't let go," Doctor Jeninson said to Jeff just as he yanked on Monica's wrist. A loud popping sound and a snap vibrated up her arm and could be felt all the way into Jeff's hands.

Jeff watched as the doctor lined both sides of her arm with the two sticks and tied the makeshift splint with the twine. After finishing his handy work, he turned back to the first injury he had found. Rolling Monica onto her side he ordered Jeff to hold her still. Jeff did as he was told while the doctor cleared her sticky locks away from the injury.

"She has a laceration near the lower part of her skull. I will have to shave some of her hair away to see it better."

"She's a girl, Mark. I don't think shaving her hair would be a wise decision," Jeff said in disbelief. He couldn't believe the doctor would shave a girl.

"I don't have the time and neither does she to argue this matter. I am only taking a small section from underneath. No one will be able to tell. OK?" Dr. Jeninson sputtered out at Jeff. "Now get me some hot water to clean this area. Jeff was about to leave when he was abruptly halted in his tracks. "Wait, have one of them get it," he said nodding toward the ever growing crowd. "You're holding her. I need you here." With that he opened his bag again and pulled out a pair of shears. These would have to do until he could get a razor. Ooh, he hoped she would not be angry. With that last thought he proceeded to remove the tangled, blood-soaked hair from around the angry wound.

After all the wounds were bandaged up and his instruments had been wiped clean, Doctor Jeninson sat down. "Jeff, she has a laceration on the back of her head and a broken wrist. She will require plenty of rest. Does anyone know her family?" Dr. Jeninson glanced around at all the people there. No one spoke up. It seemed everyone was either shrugging their shoulder or were too busy looking at one another. Idiots, they looked like a bunch of idiots. "I guess the silence means that no one knows this girl." Dr. Jeninson ran his fingers through his dark gray hair. Now he had a dilemma. She needed to rest and he had no clinic to bring her to. If he had told this worthless town once, he's said it a hundred times, a clinic was needed, but did anyone listen—no. Well, now what to do. He only had a one-room office that doubled as his examination room for those who came to him. He sat there for a few moments staring down at his hands trying to find an answer to this problem.

Seeing the doctor trying to figure things out was kind of amusing to Jeff. He knew the proud man would never ask for anyone to take her in. Just then, Monica moaned lightly and tried to roll over. Jeff reached out and stopped her from falling. It was such a pitiful sight that Jeff decided right there and then to take her home with him.

"Look, I don't know where she came from or who she is, but we need to get her out of the cold. I'll take her to my place. I have plenty of room and I have no doubts that Mrs. Thomas would love to have a girl to look after." Jeff looked at the smiling face of the doc. "If it's all right with you?"

"That would be a splendid idea and I thank you for doing so."

"Can you get your driver to bring us to my house? My drivers not due back to get me for another hour," Jeff gingerly asked, after all the doctor had treated this wondrous creature without asking for one penny. He was sure the money issue would surface later and he would gladly take care of it if she were unable to.

Doctor Jeninson rose up and walked over to the door and yelled out. "Driver, bring Mr. Morris to his residence and be careful, he has an injured companion." By this time the crowd had separated in order for Jeff to carry his precious bundle past them. The driver was already set and opened the door for his passengers. Jeff placed her on the seat next to him and replaced his bloodstained jacket with a knitted blanket that was on the opposite seat. The doctor definitely liked to stay warm, there were at least three other blankets of various sizes and colors. He sincerely hoped that the top one was not his favorite because the wound on the back of her head was still bleeding and was sure to stain it.

I WILL HAVE YOU!

The trip only took about twenty minutes at a cautious pace to reach his home. He lived on the outskirts of town where it was quiet. Jeff never cared for the hustle and bustle of nighttime commuters and bar hoppers. The streets would get littered with drunks and gun crazed maniacs. No thank you. He didn't want any part of that. He liked it just fine out here. Seeing that his house was approaching he lifted Monica into his arms and waited for the driver to open the door. Just as it did open, Jeff bounded out of the carriage on swift feat and sprinted up the stairs to the front door.

The driver raced ahead of him without being asked and started tugging the bell rope frantically. Mrs. Thomas opened the door just as Jeff was about to kick it in.

Startled, Mrs. Thomas leaned back in order to give Jeff a wide birth. "Oh my, " she exclaimed, placing her hand on her chest.

"Make a room ready, women, now," Jeff shouted. Mrs. Thomas ran up the stairs as fast as her old legs would let her. Just as he reached the top, Jeff yelled out to her to open his old room. He would place her in there. The extra-added weight did not make it easy to ascend the staircase, so he quickened his pace. He rushed through the doorway of his old room and placed his delicate bundle on the bed where Mrs. Thomas has pulled back the sheets and fluffed the pillows.

Turning to Mrs. Thomas, Jeff spoke quite plainly. "Do not let her get up and if she awakes, try to keep her calm." Jeff reached into his pocket and handed her a little brown bottle, "Here, this is laudanum. It is for her pain. If she does wake up and her pain is too much, mix one portion of it with three portions of water and have her drink it." Jeff took one last glance at Monica before he turned and walked over to the door.

"One last thing Mrs. Thomas. I still have some unfinished affairs to attend to. I will be back soon. Take good care of her." With that he softly shut the door and left his new charge with his most trusted help.

Chapter 16

"Monica, I'm home," Charles yelled out as he walked in the door. Glancing around the room as he took a seat in his tall back brown chair that was next to the door. As he was removing his well-worn leather jacket, it dawned on him that no answer had come in reply to his announcement. That was strange, Monica was always waiting for him. He had come to appreciate and to almost expect her to greet him home with a kiss, as had been their routine.

"Monica, are you home?"

Again no answer, only his voice echoing through their small empty house. Standing up, Charles walked across the living room and silently opened the bedroom door. Maybe she had decided to take an evening nap. Charles peeked his head around the door and scanned the room. The bed was still a mess from the night before. The blankets were tossed into the middle and still remained there from this morning. Plus, clothes were still on the end on the bed. It certainly looked as if nothing had been done all day in here. Charles started to feel a little worried. Monica had always been very picky about presentation, even in a room where no one else would visit. Baffled, Charles turned and left the room.

Walking back into the living room, he glanced into the kitchen. The breakfast dishes were still on the table and there was no sign that any other plates of food were made that day. He looked toward the wall where the coats usually hung on a hanger and her winter coat was not there, also the place on the floor where her shoes rested was empty. Small beads of sweat started to form on his forehead and upper lip. This was not right. Charles searched the rest of the house for any idea of where she may have gone. There was no note that he could find and no sign of her.

Charles looked up and looked at the back door. Maybe she went to Suzanne's. With that idea in mind Charles opened the door and sauntered on over to the neighbors house. Suzanne's home was not that far away. All you had to do was cross the back yards and there was her home. Charles headed directly for her back door. Charles didn't even pause his motions as he threw open the back door and entered the house without invitation.

"Suzanne…" he shouted out as he walked through the kitchen and into her living room. When he didn't immediately get an answer he quickened his pace.

"Suzanne are you home?"

Suzanne had been resting in her favorite chair in the den. This had been a normal evening routine since her husband had passed away. She took up quilting in order to support herself. It was now her livelihood. Today she had been working on one that was specifically ordered. It was a log cabin design with a dark to light fade. The fading would start in the upper lift hand corner and went to the lower right hand corner. The squares and rectangle gave a wide range of colors and textures that was dazzling. The red to orange along with the black to blue gave the illusion of dawn to dusk effect. She appreciated a variety of sizes and colors, it was time consuming and in her lonely world it was most appreciated.

She had been sewing for about three hours straight and was on the verge of falling asleep. Just as she was dozing off the unmistakable sound of her door opening had frightened her into full alertness. She could hear what she thought was Charles' voice calling her name. The urgency in his voice could not be ignored. So she rose up from her favorite chair and turned towards her dual hinged swinging doors that separated her living room from her den.

Just as she approached the doors, they swung open, slamming into her body and knocked her backwards into the small wooden end table that was near her chair. Charles, feeling that the door had hit something solid, stopped in his tracks. The sound of furniture being knocked over and glass breaking reached his ears from the other side of the room.

"Oh man," Charles said as he carefully reopened the door again. The scene that met his eyes was not encouraging. Suzanne was on her back amongst tiny shards of broken glass from an oil lamp. Charles stepped over to Suzanne and knelt down next to her. Blood was slowly streaming down from her nose and he noticed she was trying to stifle the flow with her hands.

"Suzanne, I am so sorry. Are you all right?" he asked as he fished out his blue bandana from his pocket and handed it to her. "Here this might help a little."

"Thank you, Charles, but I think that I will be fine. I just have to clean up this mess."

"You just sit back. I'll clean it up. Don't you worry."

Charles turned to survey the wreckage. Shards of glass lay everywhere, on the small rug at the foot of the chair, under the chair, and spread all the way to the fireplace. What worried Charles the most was the fire's life blood that was among the glass. Lamp oil! Charles watched helplessly as the liquid crept toward the open flames of the burning logs. Without hesitation he grabbed Suzanne by the ankles and dragged her away from the oil and hurled her toward the swinging door. The burning logs in the fireplace crackled and popped as if to remind him of it's devastating abilities. Charles reached into the chair and grabbed the closest thing. Unfortunately it was the beautiful quilt that she had just about finished.

Charles was just spreading it out to absorb the oil when a splinter of burning wood popped and leapt out of its narrow confines just to land in the oil. Flames wiggled and turned, following the path that was presented to it's ravenous appetite. Charles lifted the quilt and shook it out above the flames and just as quickly laid the quilt down in one fluid motion to smother them.

It seemed like it took an eternity, just when he had the flames out at one end of the stream it seemed the other end would leap to life. After what must have been a good five minutes of fighting the flames, he emerged the victor. He stood up and looked over the floor. The light burn marks could be buffed out and be re-polished. He would be happy to do that for her, since in all actuality it was his fault in the first place. As he stood there the smell of oil from the quilt had become stifling. Realizing that it was still a fire hazard, Charles walked over and opened the front door and threw the newly destroyed quilt out into the snow. He watched as it came to a dead stop in the snow. A small amount of steam rose up as the heat from the quilt melted the freshly fallen snow, creating a small crater. He was still watching the steam rise into the air as he shut the door. Charles took a few deep breaths to calm himself down before he cleaned up the glass.

"Suzanne?" he gently called as he stuck his head through the opening of the door. She was sitting at the kitchen table, a blood-soaked clothe in her hands. Charles walked over to the sink and opened the top drawer and pulled out a fresh clothe for her.

"Here," he said, taking the old cloth away and handed her the new one. Suzanne accepted the help as Charles tilted her head back to try and stop the bleeding. Suzanne stared up into Charles' face. The look of concern from him was most welcome. Ever since she had met him, she had wanted him. Wanted to hold him and to have him hold her. And most assuredly she had wanted to see his face above hers. No, not wanted, longed for it. Even if this was not her ideal scene, it still had some of the same effect.

Her heart rose up into her throat and her palms had become very sweaty.

"Are you all right? I am so sorry," he said as he kissed her cheek and rubbed her shoulders.

"I'm fine Charles," she said lowering her face away from his and hoped that he didn't notice the scarlet blush that had crept across her homely features. "I don't think any bruises will form. I have to be thankful for that at least." Suzanne let out a small giggle as she stood up and walked over to the sink. She had to get away from his presence. It was so overwhelming to her that she was afraid she would do something that would later be regretted.

Charles didn't leave his spot from behind the now vacant chair. He was just worried and the excitement of the last few minutes had stolen his wits. Taking a deep breath, he looked up and watched Suzanne pump some water into a bowl. She was dipping a small wash clothe into it then wring it out then proceeded to wash the dried blood from her face.

"I think I ruined your quilt," he said feeling even more horrible than before. "I will compensate you for it. How much were you being paid for it?"

"Actually, this one was for trade. I needed a new wood box. Mr. Howard down the road had agreed to make one for me in exchange for the quilt."

By now the bleeding had fully subsided and she was cleaned up to the best of anyone's ability. But, for some odd reason she didn't return to her seat right away. She took a few moments to compose herself. After getting some affection from Charles, it was like golden honey on her tongue and she wanted more, but she didn't want to scare him off. After all, he was married to her best friend.

"So, what had you so excited to begin with?" Suzanne asked as she turned around. Charles had seated himself down in the chair that she had vacated and was resting his forehead in the palm of his hands. His sleeves appeared to be crushed by the weight of his elbows on the table. She had never seen him this distraught over a little accident. It wasn't that major and the injuries were minor. So, what was troubling him so badly?

Charles knew that Monica was not here or she would have shown herself by now. This made him very nervous. Every muscle in his body became extremely tight and his head began to throb. He felt as if he was being torn apart from head to toe. It was about as much pain as he could bare. Or so he thought.

"Suzanne, have you seen Monica? I came home early and she wasn't there." He tried to keep his worries in check, but the strain could be heard in his voice.

"No I haven't. She hasn't been here all day. Didn't she leave a note or anything?" Suzanne tried not to appear to miffed about the whole situation, but, it was awfully hard. So, the concern wasn't just for her. That cut deep. All she had wanted was some sympathy from this man and all he was worried about was his wife.

"We talked about going to town the other day. I didn't think she would go on her own. Do you think she would have?" Charles looked up at her, oblivious to her emotions, he continued his inquiries. "I know she had been independent, but she would not have gone without me."

"Well, Charles. She used to go into town to shop by herself all the time. Maybe she wanted to shop alone today. The holidays are quickly approaching and you know Monica. She gets as giddy as a school girl."

"You're right. She was doing just that when I met her. I shouldn't expect her to wait for me, but I can't shake this bad feeling I have."

"I bet she will be back before night fall. Just you wait and see. I'll bet she's fine." Suzanne walked over and placed her hands on his shoulders and started to massage them. The only indication that he showed was to slump his shoulders and to let out an exasperated breath.

"I believe you, it's just not knowing if she made the trip without incident in this weather that scares me."

She should have known. He had no concern for her at all. He was impervious to her womanly wiles and her feelings for him had gone unnoticed. But things could change. All she could do was hope. She was still kneading his strained muscles when an idea came to mind. She changed her motions to sensual strokes, letting her hands roam further down his back before returning back to their original position. Then with a hint of a smile, she trailed her hands down the front of his chest. She made small circles, feeling the course hair beneath his work shirt. Suzanne leaned forward and placed her chin on his shoulder and rested her head against his. Inhaling his manly scent and the feel of his skin made her pulse quicken. She had never before taken this liberty and was honored just to have these few moments. Reaching up, startling Suzanne, Charles patted her hand with his.

"Thank you for being such a good friend. I know how close you and Monica are." With that Charles pushed the chair back. A high pitch screeching sounded out as the legs scraped the wooden floor. He had to get home. He wanted to be there when she returned home. He turned to give his farewell when Suzanne quickly approached him.

"Charles, where are you going? You could stay here and wait for her. Having each other for company could ease the tension for both of us."

"Thanks again, Suzanne, but I should stay at the house just in case. If she doesn't return by nightfall, I'll start my search." He opened his arms and offered her a hug. He knew she must be just as worried as he was, so he decided to comfort her also. As the saying goes. What else are friends for?

Suzanne accepted this gesture with great enthusiasm. As Charles' arms engulfed her body, she rested her head against his firm chest, inhaling his manly scent one more time. A broad smile spread across her face. If anything else didn't come out of this at all, she could take comfort in the fact that she was being held by the one person she craved and wanted most of all.

"Good night, Suzanne."

A feminine voice rang out just out of his ear shot as the door closed behind him. "Good night, love."

Chapter 17

Just as quickly as he entered the house, Jeff left the exact same way. He didn't even wait on the driver to open the carriage door. He swung it open, almost breaking the hinges as he seated himself.
Sensing that Mr. Morris was in a hurry, the driver took the reins and slapped them down on the horse's rump, causing the animals to bolt up and take off. The sudden motion of the carriage bolting forward threw Jeff against the back of the seat.
"Are you trying to kill me?" he yelled out the window with a crossed look on his face.
The driver looked back and took his finger and pointed it at his ear and then shrugged, as if to say he couldn't hear him. Jeff realized that the driver was either deaf or the sound of the horses hooves pounding the ground was to deafening for him to hear anything. It was loud enough to deafen anyone if they listened long enough. But this must have been the case since the driver didn't even slow down their pace until they were back in front of the Post Office.
Just as the coach came to a halt, Jeff scrambled to regain his senses

as he steadily descended the steps and waited for the driver to climb down. Jeff stood on the ground a few moments and waited for the driver to approach and in a flash, Jeff had the driver's jacket held in his vice like grip.

Pulling the driver closer, Jeff placed a well-deserved slap across the man's face. "Are you insane? You could have killed us both." The cold air transformed Jeff's words into a mist that circled around the frightened man's face.

"I thought you were in a hurry. The way you came back out, it seemed you wanted to get back quickly."

Trying to free himself from Jeff's grasp, the scared man pulled back and his feet slipped on a thin sheet of ice that covered the road. Jeff released him thus, as not to get pulled down to the ground with him.

"You will never drive for me again and I will inform Dr. Jeninson about your behavior." Jeff spit on the ground as he walked away from the crumpled heap on the ground.

"Sir, please wait. I am sorry that I misinterpreted you intentions," he said, standing up. His four and a half foot stature and his child like looks appeared so pitiful begging for forgiveness. It made Jeff sick to his stomach to see a man grovel, even one as small as this one. Jeff just turned around and walked away. He would ignore the matter for now. This man, if he could be called that, was not worth his energies. But, he would make a mental note not to ride again with him.

Dr. Jeninson was sitting at the counter enjoying a drink that he had acquired from one of the bystanders. Seeing Jeff coming, he rose up to greet him. "I thought you would be longer. Why are you back so soon?"

"Your driver is very quick. Plus, I still had errands to do and just because I was side tract, doesn't mean I can pass on my responsibilities. Now does it?"

"Mention to responsibilities. I have to go over to the General Store. Care to join me?" Dr. Jeninson waved his hand towards the door in invitation. Jeff nodded in agreement and they walked together the short distance to the store.

"How did Mrs. Thomas take to your little visitor?"

"Surprised for sure, but I didn't stay long enough to answer any questions. I left instructions and made sure they were understood, then left," Jeff commented as he opened the door for the Doctor and himself. A little bell rang out as the two men entered the building.

The first sight that met their eyes was of two men sitting adjacent of each other with their faces looking down onto a chessboard. Not even the sound of the bell ringing again as the door shut budged them from their game. Mr. Jack Parker was enthralled as usual in the game as if his life depended on it. This came as no surprise as this was normal. After all Jack was the towns chess champion. But what was surprising was his opponent. Deputy John Samuels was just as intense. The man never won a game in his life. What was he doing? He actually looked like he might win this one. If he moved his knight to E5 then the queen would take it and he could Check with the bishop. If John played his cards right, he might have a chance.

Jeff looked over at Dr. Jeninson, "I'll bet you two dollars the deputy loses." Doc looked up from watching the two men. "I tell you what, double that and I'll take that bet."

"That is gutsy. What makes you think that John will win? Jack has more pieces on the board. It appears clear to me that he has the advantage," Jeff said a little too confident.

"Having the most pieces is not the advantage all of the time, it's where they are placed. If you look," Doc said pointing at the board. "Jack has a rook, a knight, one bishop and his queen and five of his pawns. That is good, but he has them on one side of the board and his king on the other. Not a smart move."

Jeff glanced at each piece named and their location. Doc was right, the king was unprotected. He didn't know much about the game, but he knew enough not to leave himself wide open. Now his attention went to Jack's pieces, as few as there were. Doc continued to give advise to Jeff as the game played out.

"Now look at John. He only has one knight, his queen and a bishop and a pawn. They are spread out around Jack's king. With his own king hidden behind the one pawn. I predict check mate in three turns."

"All right, Doc, you still have a bet. I will stick to my original guess." Both men stood in stone cold silence while the game played out. Sure enough John moved his knight into position to be taken by the queen. Just as Jack was taking the knight, Jeff reached over and tapped John on the shoulder.

"Don't you think you should let him win and give up now instead of being humiliated."

Seeing a look of disbelief come to the store owners face made Jeff clarify his meaning. "Look, you have beaten everyone in town, except me that is. Why don't you let the kid bow out gracefully instead of killing him?"

"Kid!" the deputy chimed in.

"No insult intended Deputy. It's a phrase that us old people use to describe you younglings." Jeff, Doc and Jack started laughing while Deputy Samuels sat there outraged. He didn't find anything funny about the joking on his behalf. What are the laughing about anyway?

Jeff was only four years older than he. Now the Doc, he could understand. The man was at least forty years older than himself. He was sure, but he couldn't be that far off.

"Play with me Jeff and I'll let you win," Jack offered as soon as the laughter calmed down. "Just as long as you introduce me to that little sprat that you found today."

"No thank you," Jeff commented as he sat down in a chair beside the table. Jeff scowled as he looked up at Jack. The only subject that he wanted to avoid right now and the town gossip had to bring her up.

Spying a bottle of half empty brandy sitting on the table was a temptation that Jeff could not ignore. He lifted up one of the glasses that was resting on the silver platter and poured himself a glass of Brandy. It swished so fast into the cup that a little spilled over the opposite rim before curling into a miniature wave that eventually crashed to a halt into the bottom of the glass.

Jeff swirled the amber liquid around in the glass, staring at it as if in deep thought before bringing it to his lips and downing it in one gulp. Both Dr. Jeninson and Jack looked at each other before returning their eyes to Jeff. He was on his third glass when Dr. Jeninson spoke up.

I WILL HAVE YOU!

"What has gotten into you? Has the taste of wine put a spell on you or are you out to get drunk?" he said reaching up and taking the glass away before a fourth could be downed.

Jeff was in so deep in thought that he didn't even notice that his cup had been taken away. The image of that frail looking creature laying there kept playing over and over in his mind. Her skin looked so soft and delicate, her features with the long auburn hair spilling over her face, still did not take away from the beauty beneath. It left him feeling vulnerable and defenseless. A feeling that was not to his liking at all.

"Did you find out who she is?" Doc inquired.

Jeff just stood there in stone cold silence, ignoring the world. So, Doc slapped him on the back of the head to get his attention. "Jeff, did you hear what I said?"

"Huh?" Jeff said spinning his head around to face the other people, "Aha, yeah and no. She hadn't woken up yet. Mrs. Thomas will inform me if there were any changes that she could not handle." Jeff's mind wondered back just remembering the way she felt in his arms. It made him realize how lonely he actually was. He needed a women to share his life and he wanted that one. Carrying her was more like a deep down pleasure than a chore. He had to have her for himself. But how?

Feeling a hand on his back, he turned to face the doctor. "So, when do you want me to come to the house and look over my patient?" Doc inquired. "How about tomorrow, would that be fine? Say noon-ish?"

"Yes, that would be fine. I'll have Jenny cook you up a batch of those tarts you enjoy so much." Jeff was walking towards the door when he stopped and turned to the other men.

"Don't mention the girl to anyone. And Doc, tell that suicidal driver of yours that if he says one word about the girl to anyone, he will answer to me."

All that could be heard was the slamming of the door and the poor window rattle as Jeff stomped out.

"I wonder what brought that behavior on. You'd think that he just had the worst day of his life." Jack and the Doc looked at each other and shrugged their shoulders at the same time and looked back down at the game.

"Guess your bet's off, check mate, John."

Chapter 18

Monica raised her head from the pillow and looked around. The room was very masculine in style and very spacious. Even though the room was not very furnished there were a few pieces against the walls. A large desk was against the wall on the right and on her left was a wardrobe closest, slightly cracked on the side, and the hinges on the doors were so loose that it appeared they were about to drop off. Through the doors she could see a variety of gentleman's clothes in various assortments of styles.

As she peered around, she tried raising herself up from the bed only to be slammed back down as a searing pain shot up her left arm. For a brief moment memories flooded back. A run away horse and then she fell and…and then nothing. She definitely did not remember coming to this house. Monica slowly raised up on her left arm to examine it and noticed it was in a makeshift cast. Carefully not to send any more shock waves of pain through her arm again, Monica slowly raised herself into an upright position. Being very cautious to steady herself first, she made her way over to the shut door. It made such a hideous creaking sound as it opened that Monica was sure it had awoken everyone in the house. As she stepped out of the bedroom a robust women came towards her from what appeared to be stairs.

Mrs. Thomas had not even fully reached the top of the stairs when she heard the bedroom door open.

"Oh dear! You should not even be out of bed. What do you think you are doing?" With that Mrs. Thomas scurried to Monica's side.

Monica noticed that the kindly old women did have a weathered face and frail hands and she looked quit homely in her black and white maids uniform. Now the uniform did not give the women justice, but in the right colors she could possibly look very pretty.

"You should not be out of bed yet. The doctor wants you to rest for another day or two," Mrs. Thomas said as she guided Monica back into the room.

"Where am I?" Monica asked through her parched lips.

"This is the home of Mr. Morris. He found you on the sidewalk, just lying there. He brought you here to his house to rest. Now lay back down before I have to carry you," she gently reprimanded as she help Monica lay back in bed.

After Mrs. Thomas saw to it that her patient was comfortable, she decided to get some light into the room. Light so bright streamed into the room and blinded Monica. Pain again racked her body when she covered her eyes to keep from being blinded. As her hand touched her head, it took everything in her body not to jerk off of the bed as pain caused her to give out a painful moan.

After her body calmed down Monica noticed that there was a wrap on her head. It went all the way around her head and came just above here eyes in the front. The back was padded with a thicker piece underneath. She raised her hand to test the area and it was just as tender to the touch as she suspected.

"Now for introductions. My name is Mrs. Thomas. I am Mr. Morris' maid. If you need anything just ring this bell." Monica watched as Mrs. Thomas laid a gold bell on the nightstand next to the bed.

Monica did not remember seeing it on her first sweep of the room. It appeared to be very old and frail and looked like it was ready to fall apart at any minute. But as the bell was placed there it didn't even budge. It must be very sturdy for there was also a pitcher, of what she assumed to be water, with a glass and the table did not seem to be the worse for wear.

Monica watched as the maid poured water in the near by cup and pulled out a brown bottle from her smock pocket and put two drops of the brown liquid into her water.

"Here drink this. It will help with the pain."

Monica leaned her head forward while the maid held the cup to her mouth. It was a very bitter tasting liquid, but it did help to sooth the coarseness she felt in her throat. As she laid her head back down, darkness swept over her again.

Chapter 19

Jeff decided to finish out his last chore for the day. He carefully and methodically walked down the street and turned down an alley a little ways up. He stopped at this beaten down door and looked around to make sure he wasn't followed. He reached into his pocket and withdrew an old skeleton key. Inserting the key, the lock turned surprisingly easy.

He opened the door and quickly stepped inside. Closing the door behind him, Jeff reached for the table he knew would be to his right. He lifted the candle holder from its resting place and struck one of the matches he always carried with him and carefully lit the candle. Now, Jeff could have walked around this room in the dark if he wanted to. After all, he knew this place better than the house he has now.

As the candlelight started erasing all of the darkness, a little one room home started to come into focus. Jeff walked over to the chair that was next to a bed that was nestled into the far right corner of the small room. Cobwebs covered everything in sight. The only dust that was disturbed was where he always walked and the area the chair scraped the floor where he sat when he came here to visit. Unfortunately, the only other piece of furniture that was in the room had slowly rotted away over the years. Nothing was left of them except broken planks of wood. It was really a pitiful sight.

Just being in this room caused memories to flood back. He and his mother lived here while his father was off searching for his riches. Jeff had been the man of the family and had worked to keep food in their bellies. His mother whored at the bars in town. All he could remember is sleeping outside while his mother would entertain her gentleman friends in their home. He would sit outside the door and listen to the sounds of carnal pleasure as he froze outside the door.

The one night that Jeff had dreamed about came true. As he sat outside in the rain a black polished wagon pulled up and stopped, catching him between the door and horses, Jeff froze. A tall lengthy man stood and climbed down from the wagon. He was dressed in one of the blackest leather and well tailored outfits that Jeff had ever seen. Just as the man approached a bolt of lightning struck, allowing the man's face to be seen.

"Father!" It was meant to sound exciting, but it sounded like a question in Jeff's ears. Jeff's father had come home and found him huddled outside the family door. William lifted Jeff into his wagon and told him to stay there. Jeff did as he was told. William broke the hinge on the door as he forced his way into his own home. Gunshots rang out, but no one came running. It was not unusual to hear that sound. Every time someone got drunk they would shoot off their guns into the air. This happened almost every night, but tonight was not a drunken fool acting up.

William walked out of the house and pulled the door shut. He would come back later and fix the door. No one would know that they were ever there, he would make sure of that. As William climbed up into his wagon, Jeff just stared at him from under some blankets.

"Don't worry, Jeff. She will never neglect you again." With that done, William drove them back to the house that he now owned.

When his father had died, Jeff had found this key in the attic. He knew the key immediately and found it quite amazing that he even remembered the way here. His mother and her lover were still lying in the same position in which they had died. The first sight of the bed and the dusty remains were almost too gruesome to look at.

He knew that he would never know who this man was. He was so decomposed that there was no facial features left to speak of. He was positioned on his back, lying flat and his mother was lying on top of him. Her legs were still mounted on either side of his hips.

The beauty that was once evident on his mothers face, was now disguised by decayed flesh and spider webs. Her skirt could still be seen wrapped around her waist. The material so full of holes that it could barely be described as clothing now. Nothing but bones remained of the two lovers, stuck in the intimate position for all times.

Jeff started coming back over and over again. The gruesome sight no longer shocked him at all. He would come here to contemplate life. He had done his fair share of getting what he wants in not so gentlemanly of ways as his father had. But this time he had eliminated everyone who stood in his way, including his father.

The stairs were not the most conventional way of killing him, but it was effective. No one ever suspected that he was capable of such atrocities, including himself.

When he was troubled he could always come here. No one ever bothered him hear. As Jeff sat thinking about his next move a figure watched him through the wall where a board had split and came loose years ago. He had watched this place for years. He would study this Mr. Morris and follow his every move as he did the fathers before. He would bid his time.

Jeff was so deep in thought that he never knew he had been watched or that his life and that of his fathers had also. The watcher slowly faded away and Jeff rose from his chair.

He bent over and placed a kiss on the forehead of what used to be his mother. He stared at the opening in the front of the skull. Darting out his tongue, he traced the edges of the hole. It was the only blemish on the perfectly shaped head. The hole was almost a perfect circle

I WILL HAVE YOU!

from the bullet that had penetrated it, taking her life. Jeff stood back and glanced down at the two lovers.

"I'll see you again soon, mom." With that Jeff blew out the candle and left the room.

Chapter 20

Charles was still lying on the couch when a loud knocking came from his front door. His eyes sprang instantly open and the light that welcomed him was not very pleasing. His eyes snapped shut as a burning sensation spread through his head. He had not planned on falling asleep, he couldn't believe he had done that. Stupid, stupid, stupid he shouted at himself as he forced his stiff body to get up to answer the door.

As memories flooded back to him he sprinted across the room and threw open the door. There in the doorway stood Suzanne. He knew she must be just as worried as he. For crying out loud they were like sisters and even shared everything with each other. He knew that when they would plot something together that there was no changing their minds.

Looking as if she had not slept at all and also nursing the bruised eye and nose, she stood there smiling.

"I borrowed a horse from my brother. I thought you might need him to look for Monica."

I WILL HAVE YOU!

Charles leapt at the gift. He leaned over and placed a kiss on Suzanne's cheek. He grabbed his jacket and ran to the horse. He raced off without saying goodbye or even to give a thank you. As she watched him race away her heart beat wildly and her cheeks had a rosy glow about them. She had always had a crush on Charles but out of respect for her best friend she had kept her distance. For now that little piece of sunshine would hold her for now.

Steam from it's breath could be seen coming out of the mounts nostrils as it galloped at full speed down the snow-packed road. Charles soon realized that the beast was slowing down. So he pulled back on the reins to slow it down to a trot and then eventually brought it to a halt. The animal did not deserve a heart attack and besides, if it died he would never be able to reach the city.

Deciding to walk the horse Charles searched more carefully. About three miles down the road he remembered there was a gorge. He started panicking as he approached the deep and deadly cliff. Charles forced himself to glance over the cliff edge. Hoping not to find her lying in a heap at the bottom on the rocks. Relief flooded over his face when finally the road turned away from the edge and there was no sign of Monica. Soon the steed was rested and so Charles hurried again on his way.

Within three hours he had reached Oak Ridge. It seemed like it took forever. The wandering was driving him insane. What if he lost Monica? Would his world end? Would he survive? These questions and more raced through his tired mind.

Without even thinking he rode over to the building marked Sheriff's Office. The building didn't even look big enough to hold ten men. But crime was low in this town, so what did it matter. Charles jumped from the horse and landed squarely on the ground. As he walked up to the door a weather old man that was sitting outside of the window looked up at him.

"Sheriff isn't in town. Left two days ago."

Charles looked this man up and down. He was the kind that would not give any important information out unless he was coaxed. Charles reached into his pocket and pulled out a ten-cent piece. The man just looked at it and started to walk off, so Charles reached in again and this time presented the man with a twenty-five cent piece.

"Where is the deputy then?" Charles inquired as the man greedily took the money.

"In the general store!" he stated matter of factly as he raced off to the nearest saloon.

"Figures," Charles snorted as he walked to the store.

The door was locked to the general store and there was no sign of Jack Parker the proprietor. Looking around Charles heard the ringing of Church Bells. He had forgotten it was Sunday. The whole town would be at church, so even though he did not want to go in, he had no choice but to wait and see if the deputy was in there. So, Charles quietly, crept into the back of the church and sat down to wait.

Charles sat and waited for what seemed like a scary eternity as the reverend jumped around, screaming and shouting, about the fire from hell that awaited any sinner that did not believe. Charles glanced up and watched as everyone raised their hands and bowed their heads. One lady screamed at the top of her lungs "Praise be to the lord." Then she passed out on the floor. All Charles wanted was for this nightmare to be over. Even his coven was calmer and seemed more civilized than this. But he was always taught if you follow what you believe in then you're not wrong. So, he kept his comments to himself.

The end could not have come soon enough for Charles, but still he sat there patiently. As the last person was coming out of the church, Charles looked around for anyone wearing a badge. After about three minutes Charles spotted him talking to the reverend.

"That was the most powerful speech you have ever given reverend," said Deputy Johnathon Samuelson.

"Thank you, deputy, I hope I inspired all of gods children." With that John and the reverend shook hands and parted ways.

Charles walked up and introduced himself. Deputy Samuelson seemed to be a gentle sort, a little to gentle to be a deputy of the law in Charles' eyes. He was a foot shorter than Charles' six feet two inches and his build was that of a women's, too skinny to take down any man in Charles' mind.

I WILL HAVE YOU!

"My wife came here yesterday and she has not returned. Has anyone heard of her. Her name is Monica Flemming, Mrs. Monica Flemming. She is five feet four inches and just as tiny. She would have arrived here at noon and she has not returned home." Charles took a deep breath to calm down. He knew he must sound like a lunatic.

The deputy looked Charles up and down. The first thought that popped into John's head was that if this guys wife shacked up with another man, it was going to take the whole town to restrain him from killing someone. John carefully looked Charles over, taking time to contemplate what or how to answer this man.

"Sir, no one has informed me of any ill dealings going on and if there was a wounded women here someone would have told me. I am sorry, but I have not heard anything." That said, Charles abruptly turned on his heels and walked away.

"What was that all about John?" asked Mrs. Thomas.

"That man is Charles Flemming. He states his wife came into town yesterday and never returned. I do hope he finds her before trouble does."

Mrs. Thomas sucked in her breath and bit her bottom lip. "Well I hope he does to. You have a good day, John." The words "You too ma'am" escaped her ears as she hurried away.

Charles walked back to the main street and turned onto the road where he left his borrowed horse waiting. As he unwrapped the reins, his heart was sinking. No one has seen her or heard from her. Fear took over and his mind was not thinking logical. He walked down the street with his steed in tow. Charles was trying to think of where else she would have gone.

Chapter 21

Monica awoke to find a strange old man peering down at her. She looked wildly about, searching for a familiar face. She spotted Mrs. Thomas over on the other side of the room. She was coming forward, carrying a wet cloth. Mrs. Thomas placed the cloth on Monica's forehead. The cold sensation coming from the rag felt so relaxing. It instantly calmed her and she relaxed back into her pillow.

"Hello child. I am Dr. Jeninson. You took a very nasty fall yesterday and I am here to help you. How do you feel today?"

Monica started to answer him just to find out that her throat was very parched. She managed to raise her hand up far enough to point at the glass of water on the nightstand. The kindly looking man lifted her head and held the glass to her lips so she could drink. This time it did not taste bitter like the last drink did. Monica was able to whisper a "Thank you," as the doctor laid her head back down.

"Now to answer your question. I am fine I think." Monica stopped long enough to quiet the coughing that had started to erupt.

As she talked the doctor lifted up her arm. It was swollen and very red. Her fingertips were a little blue, so he loosened the wrapping on her arm. Within a few moments the blue color faded and was replaced by the pink that was supposed to be there.

"I am so sorry. It must have been wrapped tighter than I originally thought. Is that better? Or do I need to loosen it some more?" the doctor asked.

Monica was just able to nod her head in the affirmative direction before she broke into another coughing fit. Concern grew deeper and deeper onto the doctor's features.

"You just rest dear and save you energy. If you need anything, just point at it and we will get it. Don't rush yourself."

"So, how is your patient this afternoon?"

The doctor glanced up from viewing the rest of her injuries to answer Jeff's question. "She seems to be alert. A little bruised up and parched, but other then that, not in bad shape after all."

Monica looked from the old doctor to this man that had just walked in. There seemed to be a friendship between the two. She figured that anyone that could befriend this kindly old doctor must be just as friendly. She watched as this man came into the room and stood at the foot of the bed. He wore just a long white shirt that hung past his waist and black trousers. She was a little shocked to see his chest through the open area where the buttons were supposed to be closed. She had never seen a man with a hairless chest before. Why, her Charles had so much hair that she called him her little bear cub.

The man was well groomed at least. His hair was combed back so that it lay flat on his head. Not one hair could be seen out of place. His black trousers fit so well that it covered his lean figure perfectly. His stance was that of one who demanded respect, no matter the occasion. She found herself instantly drown to this person. The only thing that puzzled her was that she could not decide it this was a good thing or a bad thing.

"Hello my dear. My name is Jeff Morris. You are a welcome guest in my home and it shall stay that way till you are well. Doctors orders." Jeff covered his mouth for a moment to cover a slight cough that sounded more like someone giggling under their breath. "Excuse me.

Is there anyone you would like me to contact for you?"

"Yes sir," she raggedly sputtered out. "If you would contact my husband for me, I would greatly appreciate it. We live ten miles from here in Sandersville. It is the New Providence area."

Monica lowered her head back down just as another coughing bout took a hold on her. Just holding her head up to talk had sapped much of her energy's. After about three more coughing fits and ten minutes of talking. Weariness and sleep took their spell on her. Just as she was closing her eyes, she watched as a scowl crossed Jeff's face. She thought it was just her imagination as she drifted off to sleep once again.

Chapter 22

Just as Charles was trying to rack his brain and think, "Where could she be?" a carriage rounded the corner in front of him. It streaked by in a blur. As the black carriage flew by a faint outline of a figure could be seen in the shadows. An alarming feeling came over him and tingles started racing up and down his spine. It felt like someone had just walked over his grave prematurely. He was just able to jump clear of the horse's path as the carriage careened to and fro. Charles heard the driver yell something, but the words were lost on the wind. Maybe it was better that he didn't hear what the disagreeable driver had to say. He had enough stress for one day as is.

"Calm yourself down!" Charles reprimanded himself out loud. "Worrying is not going to help. You know better than this. Think, think, think…I have searched the roads, the gorge, the woods from here to home. All I need to do is search the stream, lakes and rivers. Also the surrounding woods and everyone's houses." Charles started to laugh uncontrollably out loud as tears started streaming down his face. "Get a hold of yourself," he shouted out loud then slapped himself a few times. "You know that it is an impossible task. You'll need help. Now use your brain and think of someone you know."

Charles straightened right up and took a few breaths then froze in midstream. "Jim, Jim, Jim... I need Jim," he repeated this to himself over and over as he mounted his horse.

As Charles approached the house a simple thought crossed his mind. The house hadn't changed a bit in all the months he's known Jim. The two stone pillars were still on either side of the long driveway. The house looked in good repair and even had a new coat of the tan-ish color paint that had originally came on the home. Jim must really like the color. He once stated that he had not changed the color in ten years.

Dismounting as quickly as he could, Charles tethered his horse to a ring that was hanging from one of the stone pillars then ran up to the house. He cleared the first four steps in one leap that led up to the porch. Ignoring the leaves and snow slush in his way, he reached the door and pounded. The door shook in violent protest to the abuse it was receiving.

Slowly the front door opened. It was just enough for the female occupant to look out. With the sun shining in back of the person standing there, it was difficult to make out who it was. Nancy raised up her hand to try and block the light from her eyes.

"May I help you?"

Upon hearing her familiar voice Charles stepped forward and placed his hand on the door jam.

"Nancy, it's me. Charles! May I come in?"

Nancy heard the urgency in his voice and immediately swung the door open the rest of the way. Turning away to glance into the living room, Nancy yelled for her husband. "Jim, Charles has come to call."

Turning back to Charles, Nancy took his coat and hat. "You know the way, go into the den. Jim will be in there in a moment. You can warm yourself by the fire. Do you want some coffee?"

"Nancy, that would be very good and not to bother you, but are there any left-overs? I haven't eaten anything since yesterday. I apologize for asking, but I've been looking for Monica since last night."

I WILL HAVE YOU!

Nancy felt her smile waver and her skin physically pale. Her lips began to quiver and a small teardrop escaped her wide eyes.

"You just go in with Jim. I will hear all of the details later. Oh, do you like roast beef? There are no potatoes left, but there is plenty of meat and bread."

Noticing her worried expression, Charles opened his arms and reached out to take her into his open embrace. He needed the comfort just as bad as she did if not more. "Thank you," he stated as he held her. Even though this embrace did not fill the emptiness inside of his soul, nonetheless he held her for the sake of need.

Nancy looked up and saw a tear in his eye and the desperation on his face. With that look in her memory, she hurried off to get him some warm food. The chill that she felt through her dress must be through his entire body. Pity prompted her to hurry as quickly as she could.

Chapter 23

Jeff left his house and took the carriage that Mrs. Thomas had prepared at his request. He gave the directions to the driver the best he could. Monica was so weary and dazed when she described them to him. He kind of hoped that she was just hallucinating about a husband, but deep down inside he knew that was a long shot. As they traveled along, the carriage jolted violently, knocking Jeff against the inside wall. Regaining what balance he could attain, he leaned over and looked out the window and peered at the driver. Jeff calmed down enough to call up at the driver and let his gaze follow that of the drivers instead. He could hear just enough to make out the driver yell at some man to get out of the way. He wasn't to concerned if the man heard his driver or not, but still he peered out the window. What met his eyes was a decrepit man just standing in the road leading an old, broken down horse. he looked totally unkempt and unaware of his surroundings. From the expression on the man's face, Jeff speculated that it would be merciful to put the man out of his misery.

Within a short time the man was far behind them and carriage

I WILL HAVE YOU!

carried on at a steady rhythm. The trip would take sometime, as it was about ten miles from town. So, he lay back and relaxed and started to daydream about creamy, soft flesh that made up the face of his angel. That's what he would give her, the wedding of a God, for surely she was sent just for him. He knew one thing, everything that he ever wanted, he received and she would be no different. Jeff harbored no doubts about it happening. He just didn't know when.

Again, the carriage jolted violently, waking Jeff from his musings. Reaching out from the carriage window, Jeff grabbed the driver's leg. "If you are not more careful I will be forced to find a new driver."

The look in his master's eyes told the driver that there was no humor in this statement. He made good money and would hate to lose his job. So, every turn they made he was careful to miss the large rocks and potholes along the path.

The last jolt did bring Jeff back to reality. He stared at the sky through his window. The sun was going down, leaving a bright orange hue on the horizon. He leaned a little more out the window to get a better look. As he glanced out, the sight that greeted his eyes forced him to take a deep breath. Worry streamed his face and beads of sweat appeared on his brow.

Illuminated in the dim light, it looked bottomless. The shadow from the rock facing had blocked out the view of the bottom. He started to have second thoughts about his trip home. He did not want to have to ride back in the dark with a gorge that deep and menacing next to the road. He would definitely stay at an Inn before traveling home, if one was even out here in the godforsaken land. Although he was already in his thirties, he was still too young to parish.

Before another thought could come to him, the carriage rumbled to a stop. The horses pawed at the ground and snorted in protest at being stopped so suddenly. Just to prove their point even further, they moved back just as the driver was climbing down, making him fall to the ground with a heavy thud. Mud and slush covered him head to foot. Quickly composing himself the best he could, he hurried to the door.

Jeff was in too much of a hurry to wait on anyone at this moment.

All he wanted to do was take care of his business and then find a place to sleep for the night. With that thought in mind he approached the house.

As he placed his foot on the stairs he noticed they were in dire need of repair. There was a hole in the middle of the bottom step that appeared to have been there for many years. He carefully stepped around the large opening and proceeded to take the rest of the stairs two at a time. He figured the less pressure he put on the rest of the steps the less chance he had of falling through any of the others.

The porch was scantily decorated. There was a small table in the corner of the railing that was up against the house with a withered plant in a vase. Next to that was a small four-legged stool with a faded green padded seat. he supposed comfort was not a necessity out here.

The sound of someone knocking on her front door echoed through Suzanne's house, startling her. She rose up and approached the door. She peered out of the little window in the center of her door. Reaching out she unlocked the door and opened it just enough to see out. Her left foot wedged against the bottom of the door in an attempt to stop him from forcing his way in, if that was his intention.

A very homely looking women stood in the doorway just staring at him. Her skin looked careworn and her day dress looked worn out. He could see that she did not indulge with painting her face like most women. Her skin was still smooth and young looking, despite her hair being a little unkempt. She did not speak right away so Jeff took the initiative.

"Madame, My name is Jeff Morris. I have come to call on Mr. Flemming. His wife has been injured and is resting in my home. Is he home? And may I visit with him?"

The women stood there as if mesmerized. Finally Jeff snapped his fingers in front of her face to get her attention. The sudden noise got her attention quick enough. He watched as she blinked a few times to clear her sight. He repeated his message. "Madame, again I am Jeff Morris. Is Mr. Flemming at home?"

"I am sorry sir, but Mr. Flemming does not live here. He lives in the house behind mine, across the field. He left this morning to try and find his wife. He had been worried out of his mind. Would you care to come in?"

As Jeff nodded and walked past her, she also noticed the mixed hues on the horizon. She never remembered the sky being so tranquil. This has to be one of the calmest evenings she had seen in all of her twenty-five years.

Chapter 24

Bright candles could be seen illuminating the room as Charles came into the den and seated himself on the davenport. He noticed Jim was sitting in his chair that was offset in the corner of the room. This man never changes anything. Every picture was still in it's same position and none of the furniture ever moved. The room has been this way just like the outside. The couch was getting a little ragged, but none the worse for wear. The flower pattern could still be made out. Roses and vines that were once a radiant red and green are now the color of their wilted selves, while still holding on to the beauty of their once lustrous youth.

"So, what do we owe the pleasure of the visit?"

Charles leaned forward and rubbed his face and squeezed his eyes together to try and wake himself up. Looking up, his face looked ragged and aged. Jim knew that this was not an ordinary social call.

"I am so sorry to come over unannounced this late in the evening, Jim. It's just that Monica has disappeared and no one had been very helpful in this town."

Within minutes Charles had blurted out the entire story starting at the beginning and somewhat followed the path in order. Half way through Nancy had brought in some hot coffee and a plate of roast beef that she had heated up. Charles consumed the meal without breaking from his tale. Jim and Nancy ignored the quickness in which he ate. It was understandable.

Nancy waited and listened to what Charles had to say. It was quit incredible what he had been through in such a brief time. She sat down next to her husband and held his hand for reassurance. They sat there in silence until Charles was done with the story and had composed himself again. The heartache he was feeling must be worse than any torture in order to bring this man to tears.

"Charles, first thing in the morning we will start searching for Monica. Right now you look like hell. You are not going to be any use to her in your condition. Nancy will bring you some tea. You can go to the guest room and stay there for the night."

Placing the now empty plate to the side, Charles stood up and stretched. He could use the rest even though he doubted he would sleep.

"I know you're right. Thank you. I know I am imposing and I am sorry. It's just that I didn't know where to turn."

Jim rose up and took the few steps needed to reach Charles.

"You have nothing to be sorry about. I call you brother. When I needed help you were there. Now let me repay the kindness. Now get to bed. Come morning we have a long search."

No one had to tell him where the room was. Every time that Monica and he came here, they stayed in the same room. It was the second door on the left at the top of the stairs. He turned the all to familiar path and entered the room. It had gotten dark out by now and he was thrown into complete darkness as he shut the door.

Charles took three steps forward and two more steps to the right. He reached down and lifted up the box of matches that lay there. He struck one on the wall, letting the flame light up the room before placing it onto the candle.

"Much better," he muttered quietly to himself as the glow from the candle spread throughout the room.

A chill was in the room. He couldn't tell if it was from the cold or his nerves, so he picked up a few of the logs and some starter paper that was by the fireplace and in no time had warmth spreading through the room chasing away the cold.

A light rapping on the door caught Charles's attention as he was trying to undress. Pulling his shirt back down into place. He called out, "Come in."

Nancy carefully walked into the room carrying a cup of tea in one hand and a candle in the other. Charles walked over and removed the cup from her hand, whispering a grateful "Thank you" then sat down on the bed.

"Are you all right, Charles? You look like you have lost all hope."

Raising the cup to his lips, Charles took a small sip letting the liquid slide down his throat. He took a moment to calm some of his tension before answering her.

"I feel like I'll never see her again. There's a knot in the pit of my gut that is just wrenching away at me. The more I think about it the worse the pain becomes."

Nancy again saw the tears well up in his eyes. She knew he would need help tonight, so she reached into her apron pocket and pulled out a small brown bottle.

"Here, this is a sedative. I thought you might need some to sleep tonight. The doctor gave it to Jim this summer when he took that fall from the mare. You remember that don't you? You practically carried him home. His leg was so swollen and twisted. I thought it would never mend, but you stayed with him and helped him through that time. Well, anyways, here." And she handed him the bottle then wiped away her own tears, "If you need it, it's here. Goodnight Charles, see you in the morning."

Nancy rose and approached the door. She turned just before she left. "Don't worry, we will find her. Jim knows this town inside and out."

Charles looked at the bottle in his hand as he watched the door start to close. "Goodnight Nancy and thank you." Charles managed a smile for her as the door closed the rest of the way.

Without even thinking twice, Charles popped the cork off of the little bottle. The smell was not exactly appealing, but if he were to get some sleep he would have to use the medicine. He carefully tilted the bottle, letting a couple of drops drip down into his tea.

It only took a few minutes for the medicine to start working once he finished his tea. His mind became very foggy and the room had started to become a blur in his mind. He laid his head back onto his pillow and closed his eyes. Thoughts of Monica lost and frightened soared through his minds eyes before he drifted off to sleep.

Chapter 25

As Jeff started waking up, last night's memories came flooding back to him. He went to sit up just to find an arm over his chest. Careful not to wake up his sleeping companion he slide sideways out from under her possessive hold. When her hand fell clear, he proceeded to get out of bed and walked down the stairs and into the den. Jeff stood there for a moment in his nakedness staring at the disheveled clothing still lying in a pile on the davenport where they had been discarded last night.

"Well I still have the touch," he boasted to himself. He was just so proud of himself. After their first bout of lovemaking they had a light snack in the kitchen. Suzanne had unintentionally informed Jeff about all of Monica's likes and dislikes. She told of Monica's birthday and that she was a rich heiress. Suzanne loved to tell stories of the past and also of the present, especially if the story involved Charles. She even mentioned about the fire last night and how she was saved. Jeff had noticed how her face lightened up every time she mentioned Charles's name. This had become very interesting to Jeff, even now he was plotting on how to use any of the information.

Jeff walked over to the stove and stoked a fire and put on the peculator for coffee. He noticed that there was no more wood in her box. Walking to the window he glanced out and saw stacks of wood by the outhouse. Well, he might as well knock out two things at one time. Jeff hurriedly dressed and steeled himself against the cold. How he missed his chamber pots. He had not had to go outside for his private business since he was a child. So, with one last breath he raced out and into the cold. Jeff kicked the door back open and dropped the arm full of wood that he had gathered down by the stove. Kindness can get more information than anything else. Jeff poured a cup of coffee that had finished brewing while he was outside. He actually surprised himself. He had not had to do it for himself in over twenty years and was shocked to realize he still remembered and as a bonus the coffee was actually better than that of his maids. *The spoils are actually better when you do them yourself*, he thought to himself.

Seeing Suzanne enter the room pulled Jeff out of his self-indulged daydreaming. He looked up from his cup and smiled at her. She breezed in wearing a green flowered dress that was actually very plain, but at least is was better than what she had on when he arrived. He did notice one thing about her this morning. She was very bright and cheerful, you could say she was glowing.

"Good morning, sir," she greeted him.

"And good morning to you, dear lady."

"Did you sleep well?" she inquired as she poured herself a cup of coffee and then sat down next to Jeff at the table.

He took a break from blowing on his coffee to peer over at her. "I slept very well, thank you," he said with a smirk on his face and winked at her causing her face to blush. Sipping his coffee he glanced over the rim of his cup and contemplated on how to work her into his plans. She was already wrapped around his finger, all he had to do was call and she would be there. "My driver will be here soon, would you like to go into town with me and see Monica and hopefully find Charles?"

A smile brightened her face and a small giggle escaped her lips.

She hadn't been to town in months, it came as a welcome invitation. Ooh, she could get Charles out of the cold and help him. His gratitude would be so great that he would be indebted to her. That thought raced through her head so quickly that Monica being hurt had not even mattered to her. She admitted that she felt a little guilty over that fact, but she couldn't bring herself to worry about Monica. Her sole concentration was over Charles being out in the cold.

"Suzanne, did you hear what I said?"

"Huh, oh I am sorry, Jeff. I was just taken back by the invitation. Of course I will accompany you. Monica would be pleased to see a familiar face. Thank you."

"Well go pack a bag that will last a few days. I don't know when we will get back here."

Suzanne turned and ran up the stairs without looking back. Jeff stood up and watched her depart. He knew she was not shocked about being asked to join him, but he was not going to tell her that, he could read her like a book. She was going to be easy to use. He would save that piece of information for himself. It could come in handy, at least he would know when she was lying.

Excitement raced through her so bad that she did not even notice that she was not packing matching under things for her dresses. The idea of helping Charles was so intense she paid no heed to what toiletries were packed either. One thought kept popping into her mind. If Monica died from her injuries, he would be hers. A small spark of hope steadied her hands as she closed up the decrepit bag. One day he would be hers. She would make…

"Suzanne, my driver's here," Jeff yelled up, breaking her concentration.

Hearing footsteps coming down the stairs was Jeff's cue that all was ready. So he just turned around and walked out and got into his carriage. It didn't take long for Suzanne to lock up and join him in the carriage. After a few moments she watched as her home slipped further and further away as a quivering feeling grew stronger in the pit of her being. This was turning out to be more promising than she had imagined.

Chapter 26

Charles's head rolled back and forth on the pillow trying to escape the annoying sound in the room. It sounded like fifty drums beating in unison. "Charles are you awake," Nancy called from behind the door.

He could vaguely make out the voice calling to him. In his drugged state of mind, everything seemed louder and more like gibberish. Slowly, he forced one of his eyes open. He lay there just staring straight up, trying to focus on the ceiling. Thankfully the light coming in was still dim through the heavy drapes that covered the windows. Sunlight would have been his worst enemy right now.

Another round of drumming met his ears for a second time, causing him to flinch with each beat. The vibration was so bad that Charles sat up. This time he heard the gentle call from the door.

"Charles, are you awake? It's time to get up…"

"Come on in, Nancy. I'm up."

Nancy carefully walked in so she wouldn't spill the cup of hot coffee that she was carrying.

"I figured you could use this. It will help you wake up," she said as she placed the steaming cup on the nightstand by the bed. Pushing himself to a more comfortable sitting position, Charles picked up the cup and gratefully smiled over at Nancy. The generous offer was much needed to clear his foggy mind.

"Thanks, Nancy. You know that I really didn't mean to impose on you like this. I really appreciate you taking me in last night."

"You and Monica are our best friends and Jim and I know that if we were in a similar predicament, you would not hesitate to do the same. You of all people have already proven that time and time again. No thanks are needed from you. You're family and that's all that matters."

"That we would Nancy, that we would. Just like you, we would help without hesitation." For the first time since entering the room, Nancy noticed that Charles was naked under his sheets.

"I better go down and see to breakfast. I'll get Jim and you two can talk over what you're going to do." With that said, she rose up and quietly left the room.

Chapter 27

The trip home had turned out to be more exhausting than Jeff had predicted. It turned out that Suzanne was more of a talker than Jeff had originally thought and that could be very dangerous for his plans. But for now he would learn everything he could about Monica. He would absorb all the information to memory and later apply all the information for his own use.

Jeff had decided to head directly for home. He believed a bath and a change of clothes might revitalize him. It had been a long and cold journey and he was starting to feel a little tired and aggravated. Even though he was learning more than he wanted about her husband, her raspy voice did have a way of attacking the head and causing pain after a while.

Relief flooded over Jeff as his home came into view. It was the first time he felt welcomed by this sight. It would be good to get a little separation from his bothersome companion. She talked more about situations that included Charles then she did about Monica. Finally Jeff was so frustrated that he bluntly asked, "Are you in love with Charles?"

Suzanne immediately lowered her eyes and rocked her head back and forth in denial and whispered a weak "No."

He knew she would deny it. Despite her feelings, Monica was still her best friend. It's one thing that Jeff had to admit, she stayed loyal on the outside and this did impress him a little, but in the same instance troubled him as well. Could he really trust her with his plan to try and keep Monica for himself.

"Sir, I do believe you have company. There's a carriage in the drive."

Hearing the driver yell something inaudible above the clopping of hooves on stone, Jeff peered out the window. There was a carriage in his drive. He automatically recognized it as one of the carriages "For Hire" from town. Confusion marked his face, he wasn't expecting anyone until later that evening.

As the carriage came to a halt, Jeff unceremoniously leapt from his carriage into a mud hole, splattering water and muck all over his socks and breeches, completely drenching his shoes. His already bad mood did not lend any help when he grabbed the other driver by his shirtfront and pulled him close enough to smell his foul breath.

"Whom are you waiting for?" Jeff growled while still looking into the terrified eyes of the rent-a-driver.

"I do apologize for blocking your drive, sir," the man stammered. "The gentlemen I brought sez his wife is in yur house here, sir." Jeff threw the man away from him without taking note of his lack of education in his speech.

Jeff raised his hand to cut off the rest of this pitiful mans muttering. "Well, well. I guess we do not have to continue our search for the elusive husband. It seems he has found what he was searching for, Miss Suzanne."

Jeff assisted Suzanne out of the carriage and without another word turned away and walked from his lady companion and opened the door and walked in without escorting her properly. Suzanne turned and followed right behind her courtly gentleman and entered the foreboding house without invitation.

Mrs. Thomas was just coming down the newly painted staircase when the front door opened abruptly. The worried look and lips pursed together in fear just made the situation a little amusing to Jeff. The surly women, wringing her hands in her apron expecting to be reprimanded for allowing strangers in, was a sight. Small amounts of sweat beads were appearing on her upper lip and she looked on in fear. Jeff knew he could be formidable but he didn't think he ever gave this women trouble enough to fear him. He would have to talk to her later, right now there were other pressing matters.

"Mr. Morris…" she blurted out, "I couldn't stop him, sir. He …"

Jeff reached out and put his hands on her arms. "It's all right. You did not do anything wrong."

With an outward sigh of relief, Mrs. Thomas continued to look mortified.

"Where is her husband now."

"He is upstairs sir with the Deputy and another man. They are watching over Monica. She woke earlier for a few minutes and is now sleeping from the medicine the doctor gave her."

"Would you please prepare some food for our guests and tell that "for hire" driver out there that he is no longer required and pay the tab as well."

"Yes, sir." Mrs. Thomas hesitated a moment when a very petite women came up from behind her employer and stood near him as if she belonged. She would inquire later about it. She then turned and raced off to do her chore. Mr. Morris was sure taking this well. When he left yesterday he was in such a state. What had changed his mood overnight she mussed as she went about her business.

Chapter 28

Jeff altered his plans because of the unexpected visitors. Unexpected, huh, that's a joke, deep down he knew the husband would be around but did not know it would be this soon. He had hoped to have some time alone with the enchanting female that piqued at his interest. Her high cheeks with closed eyes held him in a trance. Even now when she was in a different room he could still see her face as if she was right there. His entire insides trembled as he washed his face and redressed in clean clothes.

After finishing his grooming, Jeff stood in front of the mirror looking at his appearance. He wanted every hair in place so that when she awoke, he too would pique her interest as she had his. Looking over his shirt and vest he decided to make a change first before going upstairs.

Charles was sitting on the bed staring down into Monica's face when a light rapping sounded from the door. Charles stood and thinking it was the maid he swung the door open. The face that greeted him was not what was expected and it took him by surprise causing him to take a few steps back. Charles' faltering allowed an opening that Jeff could not resist.

Stepping into the opening that was made, Jeff approached the bed and stared into the vision of beauty that lay in his bed. Darkened lines under her eyes spoke volumes of her frailty. Jeff looked over her wrapped wrist and took notice that clean bandages were applied. Jeff smiled to himself. Mrs. Morris has been taking very good care of her and that pleased him. It took every ounce of will power Jeff possessed to turn to the man in the room.

They were about the same height but while Charles was darker than his fair complexion, the power and strength emanating from him could not be ignored. Charles was a man that one did not take on lightly without a plan of action. He reminded him of himself. Jeff would take note and search for any weaknesses.

"Good day sir," Jeff matter-of-factly stated as he extended out his hand. "My name is Jeff Morris. Your humble host. I must say, it was quit a surprise to find you in my home. I had left yesterday in search of you at your wife's request."

Charles accepted the extended hand and noticed that it was not the handshake of a weakling as he had anticipated. "Sir, I do apologize for barging in the way I did. I'm afraid my ungentlemanly introduction may have frightened your housemaid beyond repair. I fear she has been ignoring me since my arrival." Charles released Jeff's hand and went back to sit by Monica's side. The look of sadness washed over his face as he pushed back a loose strand of hair from the side of her face.

"What happened to her?"

Jeff stood at the end of the bed leaning against one of the four posters that rose almost to the ceiling. Slowly he explained what had happened that had brought the lady into his keeping, He kept any emotional meanings or notions out of his speech and tone. As Jeff finished his story and glanced over at Charles, he noted a tear slipping down his face. So he did have a weakness. But this one he could understand, since he had held her he was compelled to hold her and protect her. Unlike Charles though, he intended to keep that weakness a secret from this man.

Charles removed the blanket from the areas that Jeff had named where all injuries were found. He wanted to do a more thorough search but he did not dare with the stranger looking on. He would not put his wife in a complicated situation by allowing another man view her body as she lay helpless. Raising her splinted hand gently so as not to hurt her, he scanned her bruised skin that surrounded her bandages. Looking at her fingers, he inwardly cringed and turned to his host.

"Not to be ungrateful, but where is her wedding ring?"

Jeff blinked at that question. Where did that come from? Jealousy or just simple inquiry. Jeff felt the circle of metal in his pocket and did not hesitate to answer. "Sir, to be honest, I do not know. In all of the excitement and people around when we were trying to bandage the hand. I remember it was removed, but I do not know where it was placed. I am sorry. I will endeavor to look for it."

Jeff put on his best face and prayed that he looked honest enough. He did not want to think of her as married and to see a ring on her hand was more than he could bare. This thought did bother him for he had everything he could want why would it matter if this woman was married. He could have any women in the saloon or anywhere else for that matter. Glancing down at the women lying in the bed brought back the stirring in his loins, making it hard to stand in his tailored breeches. Jeff looked back at Charles and decided that they should leave the room before his condition was evident to this man that was slowly becoming his enemy.

"Why don't we go downstairs for dinner and let her rest. By the way," Jeff said, glancing around the room, "where are your friends? The maid said that the Deputy and another gentleman was here."

"They had to leave. Jim had to get back to his wife before she started to panic and the Deputy had patrols. With his job done, I guess he had no other reason to stay." Charles glanced back at his sleeping wife. She would probably sleep for another hour or two and he would be in no shape if he neglected himself as well. Charles allowed himself to be led out the door.

Sensing Charles' distress, Jeff turned and shut the bedroom door to block her from his sight. "She'll be fine. Mrs. Morris has not had anyone to pamper in a long time and she is enjoying playing a motherly role right now. She will call us if your wife happens to wake. Come, dinner is waiting."

"I just wanted to say thank you, Jeff. I don't know what I would do if anything was to happen to her, she is my life."

"Oh, no thanks are necessary. I think anyone in this town would have done the same."

Charles lowered his head and shook the sadness away. She was fine and already had a doctor caring for her. Everything would be fine. Taking in a deep breath to calm himself, he felt the wait and worry of the past day slip away.

"How much did the doctor charge? I would like to make sure that everything is paid back in full and I would also like to compensate you for your time and the use of your room."

Jeff looked up and mussed over the offer. Scoffing inwardly at the offer. He would have done this kind gesture for this woman regardless. "You do not owe me anything," Jeff stated a little too flatly. "I like to help when I can." That lie slipped past his lips with an ease that he did not know he possessed. "The amount is minuscule and would not even bother me. Don't give that another thought. Let's sit and have supper."

With that said Jeff led them to the dining room where they took their seats and ate the scrumptious meal that Mrs. Morris had prepared in silence.

Chapter 29

From his hiding place among the well-manicured shrubs, the stout little man watched in silence. He was just about to place another note for poor little Jeff to find and muse over when a carriage had sped into the drive and three men exited, forcing him to quickly hide.

A quizzical look crossed his face as he watched the first of the men barge into the house. He could hear their voices, but could not make out what was being said. He cocked his head to the side and watched as he noted that one of the men was the Deputy from town. Puzzled he watched until they disappeared into the house.

What could have happened that would have had the law involved? This was not in his plans. The law be damned this was his revenge. The first was taken from him when he watched Jeff kill his father and now he planned on taking his revenge on the son of a bitch for taking what was rightfully his. No one was supposed to kill William Morris but himself. Fury built up inside of him just remembering the sight of Jeff walking away from the gruesome sight that he himself was supposed to have caused. Now, his revenge still unabated he would have to bide his time again and take out the full fury on the despicable cad that stole the one purpose in his life. He had plotted and planned for five years, waiting for William to come back to town and just when he had what he wanted in his grasp it slipped away. This time he would not let it slip away. But with the law around he would have to work more slowly and be very careful. He may be planning murder but he would not go to jail for the bastard.

With new resolve he held his position. After a few minutes and no one came back into sight, he was about to step out and try to go over to the window and see if he could get a hint of what was happening when a second carriage rounded the house and stopped suddenly. He stepped back and crouched down again as he caught sight of the one person that he could relate to. He knew that stature and walk anywhere, Mr. Morris the younger.

He watched as the man leapt down and man handled the driver of the other carriage then stormed into his home. His eyebrow quirked up as he saw a homely looking women follow cautiously behind. He could not divert his eyes as he watched her walk in without a greeting or invitation and was puzzled when she stepped just into the doorway and stopped. She appeared to be frozen in place.

Curiosity was starting to get the best of him. If nothing else happened in a few he would try again to approach the house. It did not take too long before he saw Mrs. Thomas come out of the house and pay the driver of the other carriage and bid him off. She then turned back and went into the house, closing the door behind her. The women inside only shifted enough to allow the door to breeze past her and then she returned to her original position. Pulling his hood further down over his face, the stout figure stayed crouched behind the bushes.

"Maybe, I should just go around back and have my wife place the note," he mussed out loud.

"No. She might slip up and let it leak that he was behind the other notes." He couldn't afford that.

Just thinking of his wife Jenny in that house cooking for that man made a smile come to his lips. When this was done he planned on going home and marrying into position that more befitted him. This ruse of a marriage was nice and did have some benefits. He did have a little regret, he really did come to at least like her, but she is not what his mother would approve of. He had never disappointed her and he wouldn't start now.

It was hard enough writing home with the news that the man, whom he was there to kill, was killed by another. His mother had wrote back that it was his job to take out the man that let the opportunity slip from him. He did not have to be told what that meant. When he read that he was saddened. Was her anger so deep that the death of the man was not enough? She wanted the son dead as well. He knew she had a right and it was the son's responsibility to make wrongs right and he knew it. He did feel cheated and would do as asked.

Not seeing any motion or any doors open for some time, he took the chance and raced over to the tall trees that were placed around the grounds below the great windows. Rising to his tiptoes he peered into the windows. He glanced into the large drawing room where Mrs. Thomas and this odd women were sitting having tea as if it was second nature. He stayed and watched as Mrs. Thomas rose up and left. A few minutes later the Deputy and the other man left in Jeff's carriage.

Mrs. Thomas appeared again and led the women from the room and watched as they headed towards the stairway. She must be a guest to be guided upstairs. Jeff rarely had guests and if he did, none stayed all night, not even the floozies that would frequent to satisfy the carnal cravings of that man. He would send them away when he was done with them and not even look back as they left the room.

What a strange line of events. First, visitors barge in, two leave and one stays. Then this strange woman appears and is welcomed like a family member. How odd! He wished he could hear what was going on. Maybe if he snuck around back and told his wife that he was hungry he could get within earshot. That would work, Jenny had let him in on numerous occasions and he knew she would not turn him away. She was so blinded by her feelings for him and plus he could honestly use a dry, warm place to sit for a while to heat his bones.

Without hesitation he walked around back and knocked on the kitchen door.

"Hello love, miss me?" He greeted her worried look with a broad grin.

"What are you doing here? Who's watching the store?" she abruptly said and bit her lip in anticipation of a reprimand.

That was not the kind of greeting he expected. Reaching out he put his arms around her neck and drew her to him. Taking her lips by force and she tried to pull away. He knew her uneasiness was from all the commotion going on in the rest of the house and wanted her relaxed so that he may carry out his spying without her taking notice of it.

"The store is fine. Little Timothy is watching it, nothing ever happens and he is a good worker. Second, can't a husband miss his wife." With that he pulled her a little more gently into his arms and felt her physically give in. Her lips softened and opened for his much-needed kiss. It had been so stressful since that little wisp of a girl was carried in the day before and her normal schedule had become so mixed up.

"Have anything left over today? I believe a little lunch by the best cook in town would suite me about now," he said throwing one of his best charismatic smiles her way that she could never resist.

"Come in but stay in the kitchen. The master has been in a fright of a mood and I have to make meals for the newcomers. It has been so hectic since yesterday."

"Since yesterday, you didn't say anything last night at home about having problems here."

"You know I do not gossip about what goes on here, even to you," she stated as she put a plate of roast beef and red potatoes in front of him. "It's just that I did not expect the repercussions of what had happened."

Jenny looked at him as he just stared at her with that curious kitten look. He was so handsome. Every time she looked at him she felt like she was the luckiest woman in the world. She, whom was a bastard in all sense of the word, and had no dowry to give and was found whoring herself to make money. She had a respectable husband, home, and a job and no one even spoke of her past in fear it would upset her honorable husband. What possessed him to ignore the ladies whom she knew would most certainly make a better wife than she, she had no rime or reason but could not have been prouder. He changed her whole life.

"Well..." he said without even glancing at his food. "What did happen?"

She glanced around and nervously bent down beside him and slowly let it slip out what had transpired. She even related events that Mrs. Thomas had informed her in private. She knew she shouldn't but this was her husband and not one of the foolish women in town with a wagging tongue.

He sat back with another look on his face that she could not discern and waited for him to reply. "That is odd isn't it? The hermit is coming out of his shell. Maybe you'll get more popularity and get requests for meals such as this." He knew that he was eating a portion of what was to be the meal for the head of the household, but he really didn't care. He would take anything from this man, even a stolen dinner.

After he finished he stood and walked over to Jenny as she was placing a pot on the stove to boil water for coffee. He reached around her ample bosom and placed his hands on her breasts. He felt her lean against him as he nibbled her neck. "There will be more of this when you get home. Just thought you'd like to know." With that he spun her around and planted another kiss on her lips and then strode out the back door. The information he had attained might be of use or it might not be. He would probe her more deeply later when she was not under so much stress. With that he started whistling to himself as he walked down the road to his waiting mount.

Chapter 30

"Thank you," Charles stressed to Jeff. "You have been very hospitable and I know you would like us to stay longer, but I'm sure she will heal better at home."

Jeff grimaced at the thought of losing her so soon. "I wish you would reconsider. The doctor is closer than your home and my maid has enjoyed having someone to care for again and she would have someone to always care for her every need."

"Jeff, man to man. She and I need alone time. This has been the most excitement I've had in years, but there is a time when a man needs his wife alone. I also believe she yearns for the same." Charles paused as several emotions crossed Jeff's face that were not recognizable or they just passed so fast the could not be discerned. "You do understand, don't you?"

Inwardly Jeff cringed and put up a bold face. He didn't want Monica to leave. Having her here was like having the sunshine over his whole soul. Entertaining her was giving him great enjoyment and pleasure, as nothing else had been able to. He would miss standing in her room at night and watching her sleep. Her golden hair would sparkle in the candlelight that graced her nightstand night after night. The image was mesmerizing. He would step up to the bed and bend down to run his fingers through her hair and lightly down her cheek gently so as not to awake her. Once she had turned onto her back and the blanket had slid down to her waist. The sheer material of her sleeping shift allowed him to gaze her beauty. Just staring at the perky breasts, barely covered in lace had brought him to arousal. Reaching out he would outline the erect nipple so light it would seem as if it was a breeze.

He would step back and take his erect member into his hands. Kneeling down next to the bed, he gazed at her supple fairs, as he would pleasure himself. Yearning for her soft invite, he could almost feel what it would be like to enter the heaven that he knew awaited him. One time, as she slept, one of her legs had shifted to the side, leaving an open invite. Jeff took his free hand and reached up under her shift to the pleasure core of her being.

He knew that she had been given a dose of the sleeping agent and would not awaken. He could not resist what was offered to him. With his free hand he slowly reached for her. Moistness met his fingers and fire spread through his body as he heard her give out a light moan. His passion was about to boil over as his other hand moved in long strokes along his maleness. He slowed down just enough as not to erupt as of yet. Standing up and carefully leaning over his weakened pray, Jeff raised her slip just enough to expose the secret place that awaited him. He tested her awareness by slipping two fingers into the moist core and leaned even closer to taste the sweet bud that eagerly surged forward. It craved his touch and swelled under his administrations. Within moments her body shook with release and her legs parted. That was an invitation if he had ever seen one.

Jeff moved over her body, as not to touch her for fear she would awaken. He took a brief moment to look over at the adjoining door in which her husband slept and with a grin of victory on his face he slowly entered her. Her body reacted violently, she raised her hips to mesh with his, burying his member into her nether regions. He moved slowly thinking the more violent side of his passion would wake her and ruin his pleasure.

Over and over she raised and withdrew her hips. With that Jeff joined the rhythm and felt himself reach his peak. Her body gave a shudder that forced her folds to tighten around him, feeling that exquisite pleasure Jeff spilled his life force into her welcome core. Bending his head to give her lips a light brushing, Monica moaned.

"Charles..."

Jeff cringed angrily and pushed away. He turned around enough to see the moistness drip down her inner thighs. "Let her think it was her husband." Jeff mussed to himself. He had planted his seed inside that precious body and prayed it took roots. Looking one more time, Jeff placed the blankets back around her now still form.

"Jeff, are you listening?" Charles inquired.

"Yes, yes I am, sorry," he said getting his head back to the present. "I do understand. I'll have my driver bring you home immediately. Mrs. Thomas will pack your things and some food for the trip. I'll go and have the driver ready the horses and carriage." With that Jeff turned and left Charles to see to his wife.

Charles returned to Monica's side at the bed. She leaned over and placed her head on his shoulder. "Finally going home. This has been nice, but to finally be together, to sleep together and to make love again will be wonderful, so wonderful."

"I know love, being in separate rooms has been torture. I know you needed to heal, but these last three weeks with you next door...Oh, god...." He grunted as he ran his fingers through his hair.

"You did it to please our host and I do appreciate it. He says that he was only following the Doctor's orders and we can't blame him for that." She paused a moment and then blushed wildly. "Anyway, people say separation is good for the soul. I do believe that they are correct from the dream I had the other night." The last part was said so quietly, Charles had to strain to hear it. Not knowing whether he heard it correctly or not, or much less the meaning, he looked up at his wife. The rosy glow and the lowered eyes told him everything he needed to know. "When we get home, there will be no need for such dreams when reality is so much better." Charles leaned into her open arms and planted a heated kiss onto her lips and was just about to make the dream a reality right then and there when a soft rapping came from the doorway. Charles looked up as his wife and saw a look of guilt cross her face and she looked towards the door. Charles turned to see the reddened face of Mrs. Thomas standing there with her eyes down cast.

"I'm here to pack your clothes. It will only take a few minutes. I am sorry for disturbing you." Still not looking up, Mrs. Thomas went about the room folding the few clothes that Mr. Morris had insisted on purchasing for her and removed the private under things and folded them as well that she removed from the wardrobe closets. This was well too many clothes for a woman that was bed ridden she mussed to herself. Without looking up she informed them that Mr. Morris had set out a trunk for their use and would have it brought down to the carriage.

"I will miss you dear," she said and carried the folded wardrobe out the door. Charles helped Monica rise from the bed and escorted her towards the door.

"Well, are you ready to go home, Mr. Flemming?" Monica stated in her best southern drawl. "After you, Mrs. Flemming." With that Charles gave her a light tap on her backside as they exited the room.

Chapter 31

"Charles, you sly devil. Where have you been keeping yourself?" Congressman Sander said as he stretched out his hand. "Damn, glad to see you."

"Miss you too, Jon," he said clasping the firm hand that was invited. "I know I haven't been around. Monica has needed me and I couldn't tear myself away until I knew she would be fine by herself. The wounds healed slower than I anticipated." Charles lowered himself into the seat that was offered.

"New furniture? Nice color. The burgundy really brings out the Governor in you."

"Flattery will not get you away from the conversation. How is she, Charles?" he asked, without letting Charles say anything. "I hear rumor that she still does not have full use of that arm. It was a nasty break."

"Dr. Jeninson said that it looks like it is healing fine. The bone did straighten out and if she keeps using it she may recover fully. Right now it's stiff from being in the brace. She was finally able to remove it last week." Charles sighed just thinking about the nasty scar that was left where the skin had been ripped. "At least she does have some use of it."

"That is good news. We were all praying for her."

Taking his seat on the other side of the oversized desk, Jon seated himself as well. With the sun to his back Charles could not make out his face. Something in the way the man kept glancing back out the window made his curiosity soar.

"Ok, Jon, spit it out. Ever since I walked in here you have been bubbling over. What is on your mind?"

"Well, why be modest. Were going to be free, Charles. The doctors in Boston agreed that it was smallpox and since we have not had another out break in over one and a half years they have decided to send the paper up to the state capitol." Jon took a deep breath and jumped up to pace back and forth.

"That is wonderful news, great is too modest. So how long will it take once the state capital goes over the papers?"

"Well, once they go over them, it only takes a few weeks. But…" Jon turned and looked at Charles. "It could take a few months to get on the docket."

"What could cause the delay?"

This time Jon leaned up against the side of his desk, lightly moving over some papers that rested there. "Well, Ben Raley says it only takes a couple of weeks to make the docket. The problem is getting the papers through the red tape. Unlike our peaceful area, the rest of the country is divided by war."

Charles stood up to pour a brandy for Jon and himself and then handed his friend the stiff drink. He raised his in a toast. "Then a toast," he said raising his glass. "Even though war rages, we pray that it ends by the time the quarantine is lifted."

"Here, here," agreed Jon as he lifted his glass and tapped rims with Charles.

"Mention to good news." Charles beamed up and grinned. "We've been home near a month now and she gave me the best belated Christmas present ever. I am hoping to be a father very soon."

Jon slapped him on the back. "That is wonderful news. When is her due date?"

"Dr. Jeninson said that it could be around August." Charles grinned. "He couldn't be sure because of the toll her body took with the injuries. He's not sure if it happened before or after her injuries. He just knows that she could possibly be two or three months along now. I guess there is nothing like a surprise."

Both men jumped as the crash of thunder and a flash of lightning echoed in the tiny office, lighting it up with a bright flash. Both men looked out the window. That was unexpected.

"Wouldn't you know it, a storm is coming in. Well, Jon, you know how much I like your company, but if I don't get home soon Monica will worry herself to death about me."

Jon sat back down and leaned against the tall back of his chair. He didn't want to belittle his friends' pain but rushing home in this weather may be suicide. "Why don't you stay here and ride out the storm. I'm sure that friend of your wife's that lives nearby will go to her."

"As tempting as the offer is, I'll be lucky if I get home dry." Having said that, another crash reached their ears before the light blinded them again. "I better get, Jon. Keep me updated if you hear anything else. Farewell friend." With that said Charles hurried out the door.

Jon turned to his window and waited as Charles drew up his mount and raced out of town in the direction of home. A strange feeling came over him as he watched the retreating back. "Be safe my friend," he said as the wind whipped up and took the words with it.

Chapter 32

"Charles will be so please to see you," Monica said as she invited her surprised guests in.

"Well, Nancy kept bugging me to come and see you. She was so disappointed that she was unable to see you when you were injured," Jim looked over at Nancy and grinned mischievously as his impish wife pushed him slightly to the side.

"Have you seen Charles in town? Did he give you the news?"

Jim watched as a twinkling light danced in Monica's eyes. He watched as she twirled and grabbed his arm as if to dance. Jim looked over at his wife and back at Monica. Realization hit him like a brick. "Ooh, no…not both of you."

Monica stopped in her tracks and looked up at Nancy. "No…" Racing over to her friend she grabbed her hands and held them up as she gave a light hug.

"When are you due?"

A smile graced Nancy's beaming face. "September or August. The doctor wasn't sure."

"You know, I don't think he is very good at giving dates. Those are the same as what he predicted for me."

"Oh, remind Charles and I to run for the hills. Two expectant mothers. We will never live to see the births." With that said Jim skirted around the room to avoid the knowing slap he was sure to receive.

"I am so sorry I was not able to be there during your recovery," Nancy said as tears formed in her eyes. Monica watched as Nancy blinked back the tears and watched as the sadness was once again replaced by the shining glow that could light up the darkest room. Ever since she had met Nancy the old phrase about feeling like you knew that person your whole life brought a whole new meaning. It seemed as if they had known each other all of their lives and their husbands would roll their eyes when they would act like long lost sisters.

Their friendship had grown by leaps and bounds over the last five months. Even her life long friendship with Suzanne paled in comparison. Guilt over that realization hit her and she mussed over that. It didn't mean that she didn't love Suzanne, it's just that they were never that close. It always seemed that Suzanne always held back a little of herself and was not always open about everything. While Nancy would open up and tell you the way it is. She had really come to love the bluntness and honest answers. It was as if they understood each other very clearly and nothing was held back. It was very refreshing to have a change of pace.

"I just can't believe it, both of us pregnant at the same time. Oh, wouldn't Charles have a heart attack if we had a boy and a girl. Forbid if they ever married."

"Oh wouldn't that be so wonderful, our families joined in our children. That would be something." Monica thought of how Charles would take that theory. The thought was very pleasing to think about. She would definitely approve of the in-laws.

"We'll run that thought by Charles when he gets home." Turning her head to the side to look at Jim, she asked, "And what do you think of that idea?"

Jim looked from one expectant mother to the next and then backed up more. He knew that some questions were left unanswered, but he actually feared not answering this one. "I believe if they love each other as I love Nancy and you love Charles then we would have nothing to fear." Seeing the sighs of relief and the smiles of joy between the ladies, he knew he had answered the question correctly. So, to change the subject...

"We would have come sooner if the snows had diminished but I didn't want to risk injuring Nancy or getting stranded. With tomorrow being the first of April I know there are still patches of snow on the ground but Nancy could not wait another moment." Glancing out the kitchen window Jim studied the sky, "Maybe the storm that is blowing in will melt the rest," he casually commented as he turned back.

"Storm..." Monica shrieked as she raced out the front door to stand on the porch. She clutched the wooden post as she looked up at the sky. Storms always had a way of making her panic. "Charles is not due home for a couple of hours. He's sure to beat the storm." She stood there and watched as the once blue skies were taken over by angry black clouds. The dark misty waves spread across the sky, devouring the last bits of light, encompassing the earth with its angry lines, throwing all in sight into oblivion as its voice could be heard shouting across the heavens. The gods were angry today, she mussed.

Small random bolts of lightning could be seen lighting up areas of the villainous sky. As if on cue the winds picked up and swept her golden curls across her face, sending chills down her arms.

Memories of days long dead tried crashing back as she watched the ominous sight before her. The day she buried her grandmother came crashing in without invitation. She watched as the grave men were lowering the casket into the ground. It was a day much like this one. It started out simple enough, though purely devastating. She looked out as she heard the pasture speak soothing words to the growing sympathizers. As he spoke the much-hated words that would part her from her grandmother, the winds came up. "And ashes to ashes and dust to dust," As if that was its permission, the wind whipped the bible from the pastors hand and sent it flying into the deep pit dug for the grave. Lightning began to surge all around them and in one flash all hell broke loose in the cemetery. The two men lowering the casket were thrown backwards onto the dirt mounds that were heaped on both sides. The immaculate coffin plunged into the pit, cracking as it came to a final stop.

Her father tried to shield her from the sight, but it had been to late. The grotesque picture of gray clammy skin and drawn features of a frail woman would always haunt her memories. Her five-year-old mind could not process the fears and separate the two. Since then, storms always seemed to trigger that memory and no matter how old she became, the more it seemed to haunt her.

Jim and Nancy watched as wave after wave of changing emotions rolled across her face like the crashing surf. Puzzled, they kept silent as they watched her slowly back up into the house before starting to follow. Without saying a word they looked at each other and new the other was just as concerned. They had never seen her react this way before.

"I hope Charles had enough sense to leave early. He said he had business to attend, he didn't say what business, but I hope he will make it home before the rains."

"We might as well get comfortable while we wait," Jim said as he seated himself on the davenport. He knew Charles had ruffed worse weather than this and was sure he would be home soon.

To pass the time, the three friends talked about the new additions that would soon arrive. Babies were always a welcome addition in his book. They talked for a couple of hours with no word from Charles. Nancy knew that Monica had put on a false facade during most of the conversation. She did appreciate and admired that about Monica, even though she herself was worried and kept looking up at Jim expectantly. Seeing that he was still calm, helped to alleviate her own apprehension.

The storm started out mildly enough, but was now raging out of control. Lightning constantly flashed through the windows accompanied by the ever present, reverberating drums of thunder.

The sound was so intense it rattled the house, causing the windows to vibrate. Surely they would break and shatter into a million pieces, but for now they held.

Even though food was not on her mind, she knew dinner had to be made. "I didn't plan on company, so would sandwiches suffice for dinner?"

"Sandwiches would be just fine. Here let me help you," Jim remarked, even though food was the last thing on his mind, if it would help ease Monica's mind, he would eat for her. Reluctantly he released Nancy's shivering hand and went into the kitchen.

Monica retrieved the fresh ham and chesses and unwrapped the homemade bread. Laying the items on the counter, she reached into the drawer and pulled out a knife. Just as she shut the drawer another flash came through the window above the sink and another burst of crackling thunder rolled through her vibrating ears. Monica almost dropped the knife as she jumped back from the counter.

Seeing that her friend was having difficulty trying to hold the knife still, Nancy went to her and took over the job of preparing the food.

"Here let me help you with that."

Monica stepped back and let her friend take over. Daring to look, she glanced out the window at the raging storm. The view that usually greeted her was a beautiful sky and calm waters, but now angry waves crashed over and over again onto the wind swept shore, crushing leaves, foam, and any creature that was unlucky enough to be close to the sandy beach. The foam that built up, clumped together, then disguised the shorelines carnage, it could be seen every time the sky lit up in anger. Winds that encouraged the destructive waves also blew in more of the dark clouds that birthed the fierce storm.

She stared blankly out her window, clutching the knife she still held closer to her bosom. Flash after flash singed her eyes, making it impossible to see. When the rumbling of thunder rolled over her body, the knife clattered to the floor. Her body tingled and her mind felt like it was floating. No direction could be determined. Spinning, the room circled her over and over. "Make it stop!" She heard the panic of an unfamiliar voice as it screamed inside her head right before darkness consumed her.

I WILL HAVE YOU!

Catching Monica before she collapsed, Jim lifted her and carried her to the davenport and gently laid her down. As he turned to his wife, Monica shot straight up to a sitting position. Her eyes darted around the room, not connecting on anything in particular, just frantically searching till they came into contact with Jim's. "Charles is hurt!" She screamed out before falling back again and this time comforting blackness filled her mind.

Jim sat there in stone silence and waited to see if she would wake again. "She is just worried, that's all. She will be just fine when Charles gets home," Nancy stated and placed her hand on her husbands shoulder. "Right? He is all right? Don't you think?"

Right now he didn't know what to think. It had been hours with no sign of his friend. "Take care of her. I am going to look for him." Jim rose up and went over to the wall and grabbed his coat from the wall rack. Jim looked over the new rack that he had helped make. The mahogany wood was perfect for the job. Sturdy and very beautiful, it appealed to both male and female. He remembered jesting with Charles that if his wife didn't approve he would put it in his home. He smiled at the thought of the lightwood surrounded by cherry and dark oaks that he had primarily chosen for his house. Charles was right it was perfect for the setting of this home.

Jim looked around the room, glancing over a selection of various swords and war pieces that decorated the mantle above the fireplace. Monica was correct when she said it would make that part of the room look medieval. The scene was of a miniature armory in the grandest of duke's homes of old England. He almost felt a little jealous. But, when you glance at the opposite wall and looked over the floral paintings and shelves of miniatures, you didn't quit feel sorry for him. Monica had insisted that if he had his love displayed she would too. The contrast was almost hilarious. Jim reached out and took Nancy in his arms and gave her a swift kiss.

"I'll be careful. If she awakens, try to keep her occupied. I'll be back as soon as I can."

"The storm, Jim, You could get lost in it and it's getting dark."

"I know, love, but she needs comfort and if searching for him will help then I have to." Jim abruptly released her and walked out the door into the ragging storm. If anyone could find Charles it was he, besides it was himself that had showed Charles all the short cuts and areas of danger. After all, he did grow up around here. He would find him. With that resolve he left the house. Blocking the wind, Jim reached the stable and saddled his horse. Ignoring the elements he focused on the here and now and rode off without a second glance back.

Chapter 33

Jeff sat on the bed in the now overly quiet house, glancing around the room the held heaven in its grasp not more than a month ago. With Monica gone it seemed so empty. It was now a putrid well with no light that just dragged anyone into it. All these years and it had never been lonely or quiet, now the silence was earth shattering.

He needed her near, with him, loving him. The few stolen moments were not enough. His body yearned for hers. His eyes hungered to feast upon her. His soul craved for that which he did not know existed. The later really did not matter, what mattered was the craving in his soul and the swelling of his organ. Both needed appeasing and he was not a man to wait on what he wanted.

"Mr. Morris?"

Jeff blinked a few times to clear his mind and looked up at his cook.

"This just arrived for you, sir," Jenny stammered as she handed the folded paper that lay on a silver tray out to Jeff. "The courier would not say whom it was from, sir." Without another word she turned to

leave but was halted by the deep baritone voice as it called out to her.
"Jenny, Why didn't Mrs. Thomas bring this in?"
Turning only slightly to look over her shoulder, "Mrs. Thomas is lying down. These past weeks have tired her. She enjoyed having someone to care for, but I believe it drained her more than we thought." Jenny paused and took a deep breath before lowering her eyes. "I believe, sir," pausing momentarily. She had never spoken out of turn but she had to say something. " You might consider hiring extra help for her, it might relieve some of her stress." Without waiting to be dismissed, Jenny hurried from the room before he could ridicule her for speaking so blatant, or from inquiring about the note.

She knew if he asked any questions about the delivery, that she would not be unable to lie. She even wandered why her husband had delivered it. When she questioned him about it, his only reply was that someone came into the store and paid him to deliver it and according to him, money was money. Whatever he had to do to earn it, he would. Her husband's expression was unreadable and she would have inquired more if it weren't for the mischievous smile he bestowed upon her before claiming her lips with his. He had turned and left before her head cleared enough to ask any more question.

Jeff stayed seated on the bed. He decided it didn't matter where he opened a letter and right now he was not ready to release his wanton memory. Jeff's eyes opened wide as he began to read.

Dear sir,

I see your guests have gone. Did you enjoy your time away from me? I do surely hope that you did not miss my notes too much. I figured that a break was in order due to a lady in distress. To bad you do not carry gentleman courtesy in your own home. Taking advantage of a drugged female, shame, shame.

I decided to write and inform you that the game is beginning again. This time I am the knight in shining armor, charging in defense of a ladies virtue. Now I have two purposes as to pursue you.

Oh, yes. I almost forgot. The first is still a mystery to you isn't it? Should I enlighten you? No, I think not. You will see in time.

Ashes to ashes.

Jeff just stared in amazement, the audacity of the man. This was going to far, if he had to hire Deputy Samuels to hunt this man down, he would. Jeff started to rise and then thought better of it. The man knew of his secret, his sweet lustful secret that was suppose to he his, and his alone. How dare that man rob him of his memory. He couldn't hire anyone for fear his secret would be found out.

"Damn him," Jeff shouted as he crumpled up the letter. Leaving the once immaculate leaf pattern outline twisted along with the smashed textures. The ball rolled across the floor and stopped over by the door. "What does he want from me?" Jeff grimaced as he stared at the mangled ball. "Who are you?"

Jeff stormed out of the room, slowing enough just to pick up the discarded note, his mood matching the weather outside. Dark, dismal and dangerous, lightning flashed through the parlor windows as he brought it to the den to join with the other little notes he had received. Looking over the four notes, Jeff pondered as to whom could have sent them and why was this one so formal. The others were just old pieces of torn paper and this one was on elaborate stationary that definitely cost a pretty penny. Remembering its smooth edges and perfect creases, Jeff knew that it was someone with exceptional taste. Now it was just a scrap of paper all creased and torn.

The first note called him a "clown", the second "a yellow belly" and the third "a bastard." The man definitely had a personal grudge. It would not have taken an idiot to figure that one out and now he was being viewed as a villain that always received his come-up-ends. If he hadn't been so upset at the man, he could almost laugh at him. This was not a fairy tale and good guys don't always finish last. He always believed that the strongest would survive, his father at least taught him that and it was one lessen he learned well.

Worrying over the letters would do him no good right now. He debated on searching the rest of the house but decided against it. His searching was fruitless, from the fear filled attic that held nothing of his childhood fears to the cellar. There was nothing in the home and no secret entrances that he could find. He already had the door fixed of the room he broke into and had the furniture removed, burned and then ordered it buried with his father. So, resigning himself to think over the years and as to who could be so upset with him, Jeff took the brandy decanter and a cup and went into the library to read over his journals. He would find out who this man was himself.

Chapter 34

The storm was becoming worse, Charles could smell it in the air. Dark clouds rolled in and flashes of lightning spread throughout the sky. He was hoping to make it home before the rain came down. He knew bad weather was coming, but he had to go into town for tomorrow was Monica's birthday and he wanted to get her something special. He had consorted with the local jeweler a few weeks ago and had to pick up the necklace that he had designed.

Tapping his coat pocket to verify that the box was still there after the hard riding he was doing, he mussed over the special design. It was a simple gold chain but the pendant is what stood out. The craftsman had carefully copied a shell that he had given him. The shell rounded at the bottom, but had a straight top and was lined with jade on either side of the circle that held it in place on the chain. A delicate gold line trailed from top to bottom giving the illusion that the ocean itself had carved it. With Monica's love of the ocean it had seemed to be the perfect gift.

He should have left then, but didn't. He couldn't resist a visit with the Congressman. It had been a long time since they had spoke and when his attention was drawn up to the town hall window that Jon frequented and saw a motioning signal he could not resist stealing a few minutes of his precious time. Now he regretted it. The rain pelted him ruthlessly, and sharp pains seared his exposed skin as he rode. Whipping winds that would not relent were becoming a deadly enemy by blinding him and his horse.

Through the roaring thunder and the unrelenting pelting of raindrops, Charles failed to notice a fast moving carriage was following him. The jingle of straps and leather along with the pounding of hooves went unnoticed. Three miles, he only had three miles left. With that thought in mind Charles spurred the horse into a faster gait.

Out of the corner of his eye, Charles noted tethered horses and chose to move to the side of the road. He was really surprised that the carriage that was linked with all its finery and horses had the ability to keep up with a rider on a single mount. But, it not only kept up but also was attempting to pass. Without taking any notice, Charles slowed to let the carriage pass and moved off the main part of the road.

By the time the carriage had come up beside him, Charles was at a trot and was very wary due to the mud that formed along the slopes on the side of the well-traveled road. Charles wanted nothing better than to cover his ears, between the raging storm and the noise of the carriage, the sound that emanated around him was deafening. Too afraid to let go of the reins in fear his mount would slip, Charles diverted his face away from the carriage to try and block out at least one of the sounds.

A loud crack of thunder broke the air again and pain shot through his leg right above the knee. Cringing in pain, Charles grabbed his leg with both hands not noticing his mount slowed as the motion pulled the reins back. Charles looked up thinking he was hit by lighting. The searing pain would have been a logical conclusion, but his eyes met a most unsavory looking character that was sitting next to the driver of the carriage. Charles watched the rider reload his pistol. He had been shot. Not wanting to give the man another chance, Charles spurred his mount in the hope of out riding the carriage. Instead of gaining speed his mount faltered then stumbled twice before it started to collapse.

Charles knew that if he were to get trapped under the horse it would crush him, leaving him an easy target for the would-be robbers. He waited just one moment to see which way the animal would fall then leapt from the animal. Falling to the ground like a sack of flour, his faced pursed together as searing jolts of pain rolled over his body. The momentum of two bodies being pulled by gravity had propelled him further than he had liked.

"Well, the boss should be pleased, we did get him," the man stated. Charles recognized him as the one with the pistol.

"Yeah, we got him, but you shot him instead of the horse," the driver said angrily, kicking out in frustration, splattering mud all over the shooters boots. "We'll be lucky if he doesn't bleed to death. The boss is not going to like this."

Without warning the first man raised his pistol and brought it down onto the back of Charles' head as he turned to try and escape.

"Now don't say a word. At least he isn't going to fight us this way."

The driver turned and looked down at the now unconscious target. True, but boy he was going to have a hard time explaining how the injuries were attained. His portly friend did lack a sense of style but he did get the job done. "Well, lets get him in the carriage." With that said, both men grabbed an arm and dragged Charles' limp body through the mud before depositing him onto the blanket covered floor of the carriage.

"Tie him up good. I don't want to be fighting a caged animal if he should awaken." With that he took his place up top and took the reins up. "Hah," he shouted right before the carriage jolted and started to turn around and went back the way it came.

As the carriage started back, the heavily cloaked figure moved from the hiding place behind a clump of bushes. Rushing to their waiting mount, the figure mounted and followed without thinking.

Chapter 35

The cloaked figure knelt outside of the decrepit old shack that the mud spatter black carriage had pulled up to and came to a halt and watched as a now naked Charles was hauled out of the carriage without ceremony. Keeping the horse a distance away, eyes pierced that darkness looking for a vantage point. Indecision flashed around in her mind, should she run or find out what was happening.

She had watched earlier as a third man was hauled out of the carriage as it stopped by the gorge, he looked as if he was wearing Charles clothes. The steep cliffs and the jutting rocks that line the coast were almost always avoided except for the few that knew to keep away from the edge. She watched in horror as the man screamed as he was hauled to the edge and shoved over, plummeting to his death. She knew it was not Charles, but why put the man in the same clothes.

Hearing the unrelenting screams over and over in her memory, she glanced over at the shack and noticed a small opening below the window. If she was quiet enough she might be able to maneuver behind the bushes there and see what was happening.

I WILL HAVE YOU!

Between barbed bushes and slippery mud, she was surprised that she even fit into her chosen spot. Squinting her eyes to peer in between the warped boards of the dingy shack, Suzanne watched shadows move about the room. She couldn't make out definite figures, but at least she could hear what was going on. The voices were raised in excitement, even the storm seemed quite compared to these two men.

Suzanne listened carefully, trying to get any indication as to what was going on. Other than the man making jokes about the muddy mess, whom she knew had to be Charles and the sound of chains, nothing important was being discussed.

"Do you think we should have put a bandage on that wound? The bullet went into the horse, so at least we won't have to dig into him."

The man who was the driver didn't say anything for a while. "Hum. You might as well. The boss did say to take him alive. Though..." Another pause. Suzanne's heart leapt into her throat. "That hit you gave him to his noggin is going to take a bit of explaining. But, yeah bandage his leg. We'll just say that when the horse fell he hit a rock."

"Now make sure those shackles are on good and tight. If he wakes up and attacks the boss we'll be dead men."

The rattling of chains and the sound of material ripping filtered through the wall. With a sigh of relief, Suzanne relaxed against the shack. Knowing he was still alive was a relief, injured but alive. The anxiety that had plagued her ever since she saw Charles thrown from the horse seemed to melt away. Her love would live and for now that was all she had needed to know. She should do something, tell someone. She had to free him. Thoughts floated around and around with no logical plan in sight. She was never one to plan anything, even her late husband had planned the dinner parties and who was coming and what was for dinner. She didn't have the mind for it. Suddenly, she shrank down into the mud as a second carriage pulled up in front of the shack.

Suzanne stared in amazement as the driver jumped down and went inside. Why didn't he open the carriage? Surely they were not planning on moving him again. The two detestable men inside had just chained him up. Careful not to make any more noise, she sat back up and leaned her ear against the wood. At first she just heard whispering and then the sounds of boots clicking against the wood floor. She wished she could make out anything other then shadows moving. She wanted to see into the building so bad, her heart ached.

"So, how's my welcome guest?"

Suzanne's eyes narrowed, she knew that voice.

The two men spun around and stepped between their boss and Charles' limp form, trying to block the leg injury from sight, knowing it was futile.

"He's sort of out," Dennis stated. "He hit his head when the horse went down from under him." The man lowered his eyes. "I don't think he was injured bad by the fall, just got knocked out," he stated while still diverting his eyes. Dennis knew they were in trouble. The minute the leg injury was noticed they were as good as dead.

Jack raised his eyebrow and quirked his head to the side. These two buffoons were not smart enough to stop fidgeting around. Something was very wrong and he was going to get to the bottom of it.

Still watching his two uneducated hired men, Jack removed his damp over coat and hung it on an old rusty nail. Straightening his tie, he cleared his throat then ran his fingers through their damp curls. "Something else went wrong or is wrong, which is it?"

Startled, both men glanced at the other before returning their gaze to meet his steel gaze. They watched silently has he sidestepped them and walked over to his captive. Anger seethed up inside of him and boiled over. "I said unharmed!" he bellowed. "Which one of you two idiots injured him?"

Dennis spoke up first, "Ned shot him. I didn't do anything"

"Well, if you would have kept the carriage straight on the road instead of hitting every bump in between my aim would have been better."

"I drove just fine. If you would have been a better marksman as you claimed to have been, this would never have happened."

Jack watched as the two went at each other. It was amusing for a while, like watching two brothers go at each other after getting caught with their hands in the cookie jar. He watched in amazement as Ned took a swing at his partner. The jab missed and the portly man spun around and bumped into a wooden beam.

"I think that is enough."

Both men turned and looked as the authoritative voice reprimanded them. Scurrying to a standing position, Ned jabbed Dennis in the ribs just to prove a point. Dennis was taller and leaner than he but he didn't play by the books and he wanted Dennis to know that.

"Dennis, please go and settle my carriage and put the horses in the stalls, then come back. I'll need help moving him down to the cell."

Ned watched as Dennis hurried to do this man's bidding. "We don't need him. I can haul the man down there by myself."

Jack turned and looked the man over and sneered. "If I want anymore injuries on him, I'll call you." Turning away from the insignificant man, Jack commented, "Now be a good boy and sit down at the table while I have a look at my new acquisition."

Huffing in anger, Ned stalked over to the table and sat down. How dare this man treat him as if he were a child! He would pay for that oversight. With that in mind Ned watched as Jack moved Charles' head side to side.

Jack checked over Charles for any more injuries. He started at the head and ran his fingers over the back of his head. Not seeing any blood, he was satisfied that the injury may not be that bad after all. He looked over his face and lowered his eyes to look over the arms. Seeing nothing there he continued his scrutiny. He lifted up an edge of the make shift bandage to view the damage there. Seeing that the bullet went straight through and that the hole was not that bad, he deduced that it would not be fatal. It appeared the bleeding had already stopped.

Before he could finish his observations, a figure sliding across the room caught his attention before it slammed into one of the decrepit wooden posts. Not seeing any movement from the cloaked figure, Jack looked up at Dennis.

The stout man was walking into the room as if nothing important happened. "I found her spying under the window. The wind had blown her cape up and the movement caught my eye. Thought you might like to know."

Jack went over to the limp figure and loomed over her. Moving the caped hood to the side, he inhaled abruptly and took a step back. "Suzanne," he stated out loud before he could catch himself. "Move him down to the cell. Leave food and water and then come back upstairs. I have one more chore for you before this night is over."

Jack watched as they unhooked the chains and carefully carried his prisoner down to the cell he had built. Too bad the person that was suppose to grace the cage would not have the honor, but things were looking up. Leaving Suzanne lay on the ground he waited for the two idiots to show their faces. They would be expecting their pay and they would get what was deserved.

The men were back within five minutes and Jack led them outside and bid them to follow him out into the storm. "Your pay is in the carriage under the seats. Just remember my warning. Not a word to anyone."

Jack watched as Dennis jumped into the carriage followed by Ned. Before taking the last step, Ned turned and looked at Jack. "Thanks boss."

Jack pulled out two pistols from under his shirt and without a second thought, pulled the trigger. No witnesses, no leaks and no interference. He closed the door and walked up to the still tethered horses and with a hard blow, slapped the rump of a lead horse, he scared it into a gallop, which the other horses followed. Certain that they would not stop anytime soon, Jack turned and entered the rickety shack. He stopped just short of the cloak that sprawled on the floor.

"Now, how can I use you?" he pondered as he picked her up and carried her out of the shack and into the ranch home that sat hidden behind the stables. He had built the land up just so that it would look vacant and unused if any passerby happen to come across his little hide away.

Chapter 36

Charles lay still not trusting the pain that was only a mild thump right now not to turn into a full-blown fireworks show. He squeezed his eyes tighter trying to block out the flickering light that was sending dancing shadows over his eyelids. All he wanted to do was cover his eyes and go back to sleep, but his body would not follow his commands. "Why aren't my hands moving? And why did they feel so heavy?"

Charles made another attempt to cover his eyes again. Where was that damn rattling coming from? It hurt his ears, making the pain behind his eyes double. Lights danced before his eyes, obscuring his sight as he tried to steady his spinning head.

"Ah, I see our friend is awake. How are you, sir?"

"Who the hell are you?" Charles ground out between his dried lips. The sound of his own voice echoed in his sensitive ears.

"Why I am your gracious host. I hope your stay with me will not be too difficult for you. Though I think we'll leave things the way they are right now," Jack said chuckling as he grabbed the chains the held

Charles down. He had to give the buffoons credit. They did know how to confine someone, correction they use to know.

Jack stood up after giving Charles the explanation that had eluded him as to why he couldn't move. The sight of Charles sprawled out gave no satisfaction, he much preferred that it could have been William Morris laying there or his son, but for now he would deal with this new predicament. If Jeff wanted this man's wife so bad, he would guarantee him the opportunity before tearing it from his grasp, just like dangling a carrot in front a lead mule. Jeff would be stupid not to take the bait and then he would have him.

Hearing the chains rattle now because of his unwanted visitor's struggles gave Jack some hope. The man was a fighter, he would have to keep an eye on him and his little helper would be just the person. Looking over at Suzanne that still stood in the doorway where he had ordered her to stay. He positioned her just so her face would not show in the shadow of the door. Yes, he planned this perfect. He would be able to take out his frustration on this man by torturing Charles and he would appease his body's needs in his assistant just like he did when she wakened.

He relished the way she fought him and struggled against him. The power he held over her, even if it was brute strength, was superior to any sexual encounter he had before. He had shown her who was boss as he took her over and over, ripping her dress and petticoats to reach the areas that were being denied him was a thrill that seared his every pour. Soon, she had stopped fighting and just lay still. He lost interest for a while and had left the room for a couple of hours before returning to the bedroom he had left her in.

He ravished her again and again she fought him. This was a game that he could relish. He never lost a game of chess and he damned well was going to conquer the king in this one and this little pawn would amuse him for a while. He would toy with her, let her think he didn't care anymore, then attack again. He knew she would do as told for fear of being shipped down coast to one of the whore houses that didn't care if the women was willing or not. That threat would keep her in place for now. Right now she was going to be very useful.

"Monica, do you see your husband. Do you want to say anything?"

"Monica!" Charles yelled and twisted in his bonds trying without hope to see her. He turned his face till his chin touched his shoulder and looked up the best he could. Damn this position. The chains rattled but did not give.

"Monica, speak to me." Charles waited for a reply. "What have you done to her you bastard. If you hurt her I'll kill you"

Jack turned and motioned with his hand, without a word spoken the women turned and left. Soft slippers brushing wood could be heard as the bottom of the yellow-laced skirt stepped back and went up as if onto stairs.

"What do you want?" Charles said stopping his struggles. Resignation seeped around his mind. The man had Monica. He would have to bid his time and not anger him for fear that he might hurt her.

Seeing that Charles relaxed against the ground and the chains and shackles loosened, Jack stepped closer to the bars. "Now that we are fully awake and coherent, let me explain." Jack inhaled deeply and looked at his uncomfortable prisoner. "Before I begin I think I'll let you sit up like a man at least. Stretched out on the ground is no way to have a civilized conversation."

Jack looked over Charles from head to foot. His right leg was shackled to a pipe that was buried six feet down with only a solid bend above ground. It looked like a horseshoe with the open areas buried. But this shoe could not be pulled out or thrown and that was a relief. A length of chain had been sealed around it and locked to itself with a three-foot section of chain left over to connect to an old shackle that surrounded the now bloody ankle. Charles was stretched between the wall and the bars of the cage. His arms were held above his head and were held in place by similar shackles and chains. Thinking the best way to free a caged beast would be to unlock the chains on the bars and then he would give him the key to the shackles on his wrist. At least the ones on the ankle used a different key. This made the job of freeing him a little easier now that he didn't have his hired buffoons.

"Now you be an exceptional guest while I free you hands."

Charles sat up and stretched his aching back and pulled the chains that were still attached to his wrist cuffs into his lap to relieve some of the weight. Charles looked down when he felt something land in his lap.

"Remove you wrist cuffs and then throw the key back."

"What's to stop me from freeing my foot and coming after you," he retorted back.

"Remember, I have you wife. Do what is asked of you and she won't have any accidents like she did eight weeks ago. Even though I did not plan that one it was perfect timing." Jack waited as Charles reluctantly followed directions.

"Now that I can have your full attention and not have to stand over you. This room is sound proof. You are sixteen feet under ground and the only entrance is the staircase behind me."

Charles glanced past the aggravating man to peer into the shadow.

"No one other than that beautiful lady know of the entrances existence. For one, it is hidden under a grave. Splendid hiding place, don't you think?" Seeing the grimace he received as a reward, he continued. "The bars are deep into the earth and no amount of pulling will make them move. Even though you touching them is impossible, I just needed to inform you."

Charles looked the bars up and down and realized that they had to be at least ten feet away. With his height and the length of the lonely chain on his leg he figured it would be a good foot, maybe two feet till the barred wall. There was a door similar to the one the jail used. Standing up, he realized that there was about the same distance to the ceiling. Ten feet as well and all sides lined with boards. Probably to stop a cave in if he was correct. It must have taken years to dig this out and place everything in here. There was even a low stool with an opening on top for private business and some hay with a couple of folded blankets on it for a bed.

"I see you learn quickly. So, I will answer the questions behind your eyes. No, this cell was not originally meant for you. Yes it was planned well in advanced and no you may never leave. Do those answers satisfy some of the curiosity that is boiling in the back of your mind?"

Jack picked his candle up and went to leave. "I will leave you alone for now, food and water will be brought in daily and if you're good, soap will be provided. I'd hate for you to die of stench."

Charles looked up into a face he knew well, "Jack!"

Hearing his name ground out from Charles lips made him turn back. "Yes."

"I demand answers and you will provide them."

"Maybe later. Right now I have a wedding to plan."

Without another word Jack left and took the only candle with him, plunging Charles into utter darkness. Charles rested his back against the planks of the wall. He just couldn't believe this was happening. Jack? He was just the owner of the general store. Thinking back, he was trying to figure out what could have sent the man off the deep end. He was well-liked and had no enemies, well until today he didn't have any and was on the town council. Jack had been here before he had even crawled out of the woods and into this town.

What did he say? A wedding to plan? Who's wedding? A light went off in his brain, it's Monica. The bastard wants Monica. Wait, if that was the case then why didn't he take her before. Maybe he is shy. Maybe he's a eunuch. Oh, wouldn't that just be it. A eunuch, that's why he didn't approach her. He's half a man. Charles pondered other theories in his head before laying down on the itchy straw and sought out much needed slumber.

Chapter 37

"That poor dear," Mrs. Sanders commented to her elderly companion. "She has lost so many in so short of time."

"No more than any of us," the older women snorted.

Monica did not recognize the women immediately and from the way the women made their comments, she did not care to know her either. All through the reverend's speech, over her husbands' casket, this woman was looking down on everyone, belittling everyone's emotions and not caring who heard her comments or care to whom she said them.

"Don't you agree, Mr. Morris?" she remarked. Jeff glanced up at the elderly women whom he had known all his life. She was the widow of his fathers' old business partner.

"Pardon me, Mrs. Gram, but no I do not agree. When's the last time you lost someone? Hmmm?" Jeff paused a few seconds, hearing this women's sharp comments was enough to make his blood boil. "Oh yes. I remember. You lost you husband also, didn't you, Mrs. Gram? That was about three years ago if I am not mistaken."

"So, what does that have to do with it? Why does she get pitied? I'm a widow also, but did half of the people here show up at my husband's funeral. No they didn't. So why should I pity her?" she said briskly, escalating her voice.

Seeing that a crowd was gathering around, he lowered his voice to not gain any more attention. "Dear lady, your husband's body was never returned. Many of the towns people did feel the need to attend an empty grave." Just hearing this woman complain was bringing him to the breaking point. He took a few deep breaths so he could regain his composure back, it was just a matter of moments before he could no longer be civil.

"Mrs. Thomas, can you keep an eye on Monica while I escort Mrs. Gram away from the proceedings."

Jeff watched as Mrs. Thomas stepped over to Monica and put a protective arm around the shivering widow.

Jeff took Mrs. Gram by the arm and led her towards the east entrance of the cemetery. Right before they stepped under the ivy covered travois of the fence, Jeff turned her to face him.

"Now, Mrs. Gram, I have much respect for your feelings and I always felt sorry that so little was done for your grieving. I did respect your husband and what he did for our family. But..." Jeff paused and looked around to make sure they were not in earshot of the gossip spreading old crones of the town before leaning close to her ear till his hot breath was felt on her tender skin. "But if you continue to carry on like this I will tell this town about all those dirty little secrets that have stayed hidden from your husbands past. For one instance, your first born son is not your husband's and that you are no lady."

Smiling to himself, Jeff stood back up. The look on Mrs. Gram's face seemed to be frozen in time. "I believe I have made my point."

Jeff bowed gracefully in her directions as he took his leave. "If you find that your tongue cannot be civil to Mrs. Flemming, you will find it on my trophy stand. Is that understood?"

She stood still, sneering at him. "What do you know of family? Everyone knows that your mother was a whore. Why would anyone be interested in my affairs when yours are so much more colorful."

Jeff looked down at her, raised his head and straightened his shoulders. "Because my dear lady," he smiled wryly, " I am not the one who turned her daughter out and then became her Madame. Now I suggest you leave before your friend, the reverend, hears you talking so disrespectful of his parishioners." When no comment was forthcoming, he took his leave.

Jeff left her standing near the entrance with her mouth agape. She turned and left. The last person she wanted to offend was the reverend, he would give last rights over her and she wanted redemption for what she did and angering this man right now would not achieve her goal before she died. Without another word she turned and left.

It was about time someone dulled her razor sharp tongue, Jeff thought to himself. Who the hell is she to talk? If she made one more comment he would be sure that she was blackballed from the very aristocratic society that she lived for and would let the reverend know about her dark past. Jeff turned around and tucked that away in his memory for a later time as he rejoined Monica.

"Thank you, Mrs. Morris. I'll stay with her for the rest of the funeral," Jeff modestly whispered.

The reverend finished his blessing over Charles' soul and laid his bible down and walked over and offered his sympathy to Monica, then went and greeted the other guests. When the first clod of dirt was thrown onto the casket, tears were flowing down Monica's face. Glancing around there were still many well wishers about. He knew they would have to meet and greet and that Monica would have to be strong enough to get through the cemetery to his awaiting carriage.

A crowd gathered at the entrance that Mrs. Gram had just left through. Satisfaction was reflected on their expressions as he guided her away from the grave. Wedging his way through groups of concerned friends and associates, he would give the proper greeting to whomever spoke to them, but would quickly give excuses just to be greeted by another. The crowd did seem to thin and he was grateful. Monica looked so forlorn, it appeared that she would not be able to stand much longer. Glancing back he saw Suzanne following.

Ever since Charles' body was found at the bottom of the gorge, she had not been around that much. Jeff did find that odd behavior, but he blew it off as he figured she was grieving as well. He knew that she had loved Charles also. Jeff glanced from person to person, noticing that every one seemed genuinely concerned. He hoped that his look of concern looked real, but deep down he was ecstatic, she was free and would soon be his, as would their baby.

Before the funeral began and the old cronies had her occupied, he had a chance to speak with Suzanne. Finding out that Monica was five months pregnant made his soul leap with joy. That put the babies conception time around when she was at his home. Hope blossomed inside him thinking it was his child she carried. He would have to convince her that she had to marry him without telling about the baby's probable patronage. That was one secret he was not going to ever let anyone know of.

"Come, Monica, it's time to go." Jeff directed her to the carriage door and held his hand for her. He turned to Suzanne and watched as she looked back at the gravestone. He could have sworn he had seen a smile spread across her face, but when she turned to accept the hand offer to her a frown marred his face. It must have been the angle he was at, because he was sure she loved Charles. Why would she smile?

"Driver, bring us to my home," he shouted up to the driver before climbing into the carriage.

"No, not my home?" Monica responded quietly.

"You want to go to your home?"

"No, not my home?"

Jeff started to protest what he thought was her saying that she would not go home because it was no longer hers, but when he realized that she wanted to go home, he dropped his head in resignation. He was not going to fight, not today. He leaned out the window and made the location correction.

Once they arrived at Monica's home she walked into the house and just shut the door and locked it, leaving her companions outside. Jeff didn't know what to think of this predicament. He never had to deal with an emotional female before and he looked at Suzanne with question.

"Why don't we just leave her alone for a while. We can go to my place. It's close enough that if she needs anything we'll be available."

Monica threw herself down onto Charles' pillow on the bed. She needed to let the flood of tears out. The sadness was more than she could take and shudders raked her body and she trembled as natures release flooded down her drawn face. She knew that tomorrow she would have to face another group of grieving friends. Charles' coven would come for her, as was their custom. She had never attended any meetings other than her wedding with the group. They were supposed to go next Saturday, but now the Coven would come for her to bury Charles in his own rite of passage.

She had been so worried when the High Priest had come to the house to claim Charles' body and weighted the casket with stones. The High Priest calmed her fears and explained that their way was to cremate the body and Charles would not have approved of being buried. He promised to pick her up the day after the public burial for Charles' actual funeral.

Today, she just needed to let the shock wear off. She would worry about tomorrow later. Right now, she needed to smell his scent and be as close to him as possible. She curled up closer to his pillow, inhaling his manly scent before falling into a troubled sleep.

Chapter 38

"Suzanne, You have to help me, help Monica," Jeff pleaded reaching out for the distraught women. He knew she loved Charles and personally he really didn't care. He was very pleased that Charles was dead. This was his chance to have Monica with him willingly and he would do anything to have her.

Kneeling down, Jeff lowered his head in shame. "I know we shared moments. I knew you needed them as much as I, but feelings were not involved. You and I both know that it's true." Jeff took her hand. "Look at me Suzanne. Please, I can give you money, protection, and a better living if you could just help convince Monica to marry me."

Suzanne stepped back and pulled her hand from his. "Help Monica, poor, poor Monica. I comfort her. I cook for her. What more do you expect me to do for her? I have too many people to assist with and now you want me to help you." Suzanne turned away from the quizzical look that crossed Jeff's face. She was so sick of hearing about what Monica needs. If she has to help one more person against her will she would burst. Suzanne closed her eyes and inhaled deeply and let her mind wander to Charles in that dirt cell. All she wanted was to be able to hold him and comfort him but he might as well have been a hundred miles away. Jack would not let her into the cell to even tend to his leg. It was healing but she could make it heal better.

She has had so much pressure on her shoulders already and helping Jeff get Monica into his bed would only be one more… "Wait a minute," she said out loud. Turning around she looked down at Jeff.

"What are your plans, Jeff? Is she to be your mistress or do you just want her close?"

Jeff didn't know if he wanted to answer her but slowly he raised his head. "I want to marry her Suzanne."

He stood up abruptly as he watched her sink down onto the davenport he carefully sat next to her as he mistook her little laugh as a sign that she might not have the ability to handle his voiced intentions. "Suzanne, you must understand, as you loved Charles, I love Monica. If you were in my shoes and it was Monica that had died wouldn't you have gone for Charles?"

"All right, I'll do what I can. But I'll let you know right now that she will not respond to the request properly. She has not responded to anyone in almost two days. She just stands in her kitchen staring out the window as if watching for his return. Every now and then she'll nod, but its like she's given up on life." Suzanne shrugged off the hand that was held out to assist her as she stood up. She needed some coffee, before she entered the kitchen a thought came to mind. "You would think that she would try to stay healthy if not for herself but at least for the baby."

Suzanne walked into the kitchen, leaving him standing there with mouth open. She couldn't know, she must just be concerned for the offspring she thought to be Charles'. She stood at the stove pouring herself a cup of coffee, she heard the sound of a chair scrapping the floor behind her. She almost dropped her cup when she turned around and there was Jeff sitting there half naked and his breeches were undone.

"I would like to reward you for your help," he said standing up and walked around behind her.

I WILL HAVE YOU!

Suzanne did not move as he circled her and watched as a broad smile crossed his features. Jeff reached around her waist with his left hand and grabbed the back of her hair with his other. Without notice he forcefully pushed her face forward onto the table and released her waist to reach up under her skirt to tantalize her sweet bud until she was in a frenzy. Her cup crashed to the floor that she had been holding as her release echoed through her body. Jeff inserted a finger into her body until she was crying for more. Without any warning he plunged his manhood into her and heard her moans of ecstasy sound through the kitchen.

He had never met a woman that like it this way and he had always wondered if the other opening was just as sweet. Just as another shudder reverberated through Suzanne's body he withdrew and pushed his fingers into her again, but this time the fingers circled her opening and gathered the moisture onto them. Suzanne's body froze as she felt Jeff's fingers smooth over her other opening. No one had ever touched her there and she stiffened. She felt her own juices being spread into that nether region by those talented fingers. The feelings were not at all repulsing as she thought it would be and she relaxed under his administrations.

"So, you do like the feel of my hands there," he said as he entered and withdrew his fingers. He taunted the highly aroused bud that peaked out from her womanly folds till more liquid was produced and he continued to smother her backside with her own juices. He did this for a while, bringing her to the brink, before starting the process over again. She could feel the moisture inside and out of her body and if he didn't bring her over the edge again she would scream. Having the sensation of one hand in her most intimate region and the other in one that had never been invaded was driving her insane. She felt Jeff's fingers probing in and out faster in both openings at the same time and she screamed from the sensations that were beyond reality. Her head spun and her breathing couldn't be controlled. All thought left as he entered her again and pounded with such a force the table moved until it came to a stop against the cabinets. When no more motion came from the table, her body took the blunt of his thrusts, slamming her mid section onto the edge. By now she was oblivious to the pain.

Pressure built inside of her. It was like a volcano about to explode, her skin radiated heat and sweat began to drip from her brow and scream after scream came from deep inside her as her head flew from side to side. At last release came and she raised up as the first spasm hit. As her breathing calmed, he pulled away.

"Jeff, no…" she screamed as she felt him enter her backside forcefully.

Her "no" was cut off as Jeff pushed her back down and thrust his swollen shaft into her virginal opening. He had never felt something so tight; it squeezed his manhood helping him to control the explosion he knew was on the brink. The excitement he felt made him swell up to a proportion that he did not know he was capable of reaching.

Suzanne let out a whimper as she was stretched beyond her limits. Tears rolled down her cheeks and she felt as if she were being torn apart. Her screams this time was not from pleasure. She just hoped that he was quick as she prayed that she would not pass out in front of this man.

"Ohhh, yes…" Jeff growled primitively as his release spewed out, filling her nether cavity. He partially collapsed over her, as his organ pulsed and spasmed before withdrawing from her. Still shaking from his explosion, finally, Jeff backed away, leaving Suzanne bent over the table. "That was a sweet reward for such sweet information. Thank you, my dear lady." Jeff walked into the living room and composed himself before getting dressed and leaving.

Suzanne looked up to watch him leave. Disgust rushed through her body. She could feel the sticky liquid between her legs and on her backside and she rushed to her washbasin. "You bastard!" she shouted at the closed door. She had never been violated like that ever. Even the rape that she had to endure from Jack was nothing compared to what had just happened. He'll get his. She would make sure of that.

Even though anger boiled inside of her she shivered as she

cleansed of the tender areas and realized that her tears were more of shame than of pain. She had enjoyed it and that brought self-loathing to her. She couldn't seem to be pleasured or derive pleasure if it wasn't forced upon her. She would never tell Jeff, for him to know that he had that kind of power over her could be dangerous to her own well-being.

She would help him get Monica, just so he would leave her alone. She would just keep that little secret to herself. If he were busy with a new bride then he would not have time for her.

Chapter 39

Everything was happening too quickly, the gown, the guest list and the planning. A whirlwind of activity swirled around Monica. The world flipped and fluttered and seemed to never stop spinning. She watched as the caterers were set up and the dinner was planned out without even consulting her. She watched as the guest list was comprised of their close friends, since neither one had family it really didn't matter who attended, and she didn't argue or protest when her gown was fitted to fit her new form. She was so far gone with child that the waist was raised on the gown so that it held tight just below her ample bosom.

The dress was beautiful. It was made of white silk and lace, trimmed in a baby blue ribbon and pearls. The high neckline accentuated the lace trim that stopped at the ribbon that lined her midsection that made up the high bodice, from there the silk split and flowed down till the edges touched the floor on either side of the matching slippers.

Layer upon layer of lace filled the opening between the silk folds giving the appearance of a white waterfall. There was also a matching cape that clipped to the shoulders and flowed gracefully down her back and trailed behind her. The full-length sleeves were split from shoulder to wrist and opened lightly to show the silkiness of her skin beneath. Her hair was propped up in a perfect coiffeur with pearls and ribbons laced into the delicate strands and pins were entwined with the ribbon to attach a lace veil.

Monica felt like she was looking at herself from somewhere else in the room. She could see herself walking down the isle in a dress designed for a queen. Was this really happening? Had it already been a week since she told Jeff that she would accept his proposal. She couldn't think straight and the world seemed disconnected somehow. No matter how much she willed her body to stop, it would not obey. It kept walking and the music kept playing. She felt as if she were floating in a dream, her feet stepped lightly on the baby blue rug that lined the walkway between the pews of the church. Why was she doing this? Why can't I stop?

Jeff watched as Monica walked towards him, her beauty was even greater than he could have imagined. He was correct in guessing her size for the dress. He had ordered the seamstress to alter the dress that had once belonged to his mother. He had found it in one of the trunks in the attic during his explorations and when he met Monica he knew that she would look exquisite in it and he was not wrong. She looked like a Goddess walking on the earth for the first time. Her eyes were wide and seemed to fasten on him as if he were calling to her.

As she approached she looked up at him as he took her hand and wrapped his arm around her waist to steady her. Still staring at him, she wandered at the look on his face. It should have frightened her, but it did not. It had the opposite effect. It thrilled her, enhancing the sensations that raced through her already receptive body, exciting her very core. As he peered down at her, his eyes were so dense and fathomless, searing though her, piercing her soul. An evilness she had never encountered emanated from him, searing his face into her memory for all time. Such strong features, high cheekbones, lips so soft that when they touched her would surly bring her to the brink of insanity. Deep set blue eyes that appeared to be looking into her soul held her entranced. His blonde hair that was so soft, just like rabbit fur and all she wanted to do was run her fingers through it. His natural male scent emanating from his all to desirable body was like an aphrodisiac on her senses.

Where his hands touched her singed her skin, searing heat ran through her body burning her deeper being, sapping the rest of her will power away and taking everything she had left. Surly she would turn to cinders in his arms. Wave after wave of heat washed over her body till all she could do was feel.

Jeff looked down at Monica, the medicine that he had slipped into her tea to help calm her was having the desired affect. She looked as if in a trance, with no will of her own. He would have preferred it if he didn't have to drug her, but he was afraid she would run.

"Ladies and Gentleman, we are gathered here to join a man and a woman in holy matrimony…"

Jeff looked up at the preacher as he began to speak. He wanted this as legal as possible and did not want any mistakes so he paid attention.

Monica heard a tender tone in the distance but could not make out if it was man or beast, but the mellow sound soothed her. Waves of relaxation rolled over her and she lightly swayed. *What was stopping me from falling?* She mildly thought as her mind went back to trying to concentrate on the soothing sound. She felt her arm rise and light began to dance from the tips of her fingers. The flames danced back and forth before splitting into two and then they appeared to be dancing an eternal dance independently. Then they would reach out to each other, but never getting close enough to join and spread. Her arm lowered back down to her side and the flames continued to dance in mid air never faltering in their dance of death.

Jeff calmly turned Monica back towards the preacher with grace as to not let on to her incompetent state. The two candles lit to signify the beginning of a new life together.

"Do you, Jeff, take Monica to be your wife in sickness and health till death do you part?"

"I do," Jeff stated without hesitation.

"Do you, Monica, take Jeff to be your husband in sickness and health till death do you part?"

Silence. Both men turned to face Monica. Her eyes were half closed and her body swayed as if to some imaginary music. Jeff froze in fear thinking he may have given her a little too much and that she would not be able to respond. He reached up and cupped Monica's chin gently, "Monica, please say I do. I do. I do."

Monica concentrated as the soothing new tone, it repeated itself over and over as wanting her to mimic the sound. She opened her mouth and nothing came out. She listened as the tones repeated again and again, this time more demanding. She knew she must obey, giving one more try she beckoned her body to obey. The tones were so beautiful, she had to copy the sound. Then when she thought she would never be able to mimic the tones came from deep within her, sounding like the chiming of bells. She was rewarded with a warm heat on her lips and lights fluttered in front of her eyes. Then the world began to spin again.

"Ladies and gentlemen, may I introduce you to Mr. And Mrs. Morris."

Bouts of clapping and cheers resounded in the halls of the church, vibrating the delicate stained glass windows. Jeff rushed her down the isle and into a waiting carriage.

"We're going home," he said as she rested her head in his lap. Jeff turned and waved out the window as the four white stallions pulled away from the church. Finally, she was his and nothing was going to take her away.

Feeling her shift to her side, Jeff looked down at her and he found himself being aroused and fought to keep from touching her till they arrived home.

Monica felt like she was floating and it was so relaxing, she wanted to stay here. There were no worries, just enhanced feelings. Her skin tingled and everything was intensified, touch, warmth and feelings, not the memory type, the physical type. Heat radiated about her body and hunger for touch had been consuming her. She wanted to feel more, so she turned to try and touch the heat again. She nuzzled her face against the heat that radiated there, not knowing what is was exactly she wanted, but instinctively reaching out to seek it out.

Jeff watched as she squirmed on the seat and as she rubbed his manhood through his breeches. He knew what she was feeling and he would admit he wanted the same, but he would at least keep some honor and not take her till she was in their marital bed. But that did not mean he would not at least give her some release. Jeff reached over and slipped his hand under her dress and felt for the hungry mouth. He caressed it and stroked her inner core until she let out a scream and he felt her body shudder and then go limp.

With satisfaction he leaned back up against the seat closed his eyes. He knew that the sensation would keep with her long enough to get her home. Once the reception was over and they would be able to retire to their room then he would join her mildly in her drug-induced state and then he would teach her the real meaning of what it was like to feel, to really feel life, body and soul.

Chapter 40

"Twenty-seven, twenty-eight, twenty-nine. Twenty-nine knot holes in the wood planks that made up the walls," Charles counted to himself.

"Twenty-nine knot holes, round about five hundred and thirty two termite holes per board that ran from ceiling to ground and ten boards that lined the back wall. Six boards make up the walls from the barred exit to the back wall. Twenty-nine, Twenty-nine…TWENTY-NINE…" Charles shouted out as he paced from wall to wall.

Charles looked around, how long had he been here? Weeks? Days? Months? No daylight and not knowing when it was nighttime were taking its toll. His skin was almost white when once it held a golden glow and he had lost so much weight. His strength and energy was sapped, only having one meal a day was not sufficient and he felt his life draining away along with his body. Lying dormant day after day had melted his resistance. He had tried to find an escape early on but to his dismay he found this cell escape proof.

One board was just propped up against the wall where he had

figured on digging himself out and when he found nothing but a solid mass of dirt behind the wall his soul had sank. Even the ankle bracelet would not give, pulling and trying to slide it over his heel had left sores that were well scarred and infected. Pacing also left bruises on his feet where the chains had hit them over and over. His mind had blocked most of the pain but it was so excruciating that he had to lie back down.

By now his wilted body had no choice but to give in to fate. He would surely die here, but one thought kept radiating over and over in his mind. "Have to find Monica." He would of given up already if it hadn't been for the thoughts of her, to see her face again, to hold her one last time in his arms. He could imagine her laying next to him when he closed his eyes, could feel her touch, feel her laying against his shoulder while he ran his fingers up her arms.

His chest tingled as if her breath wafted across the sensitive skin as the feel of her lips spreading kisses across his neck echoed in his mind. Images started to be conjured up as he lay on the wool blanket that covered his straw bed. Flames from the living room hearth lit up the room as he reached over and gently cupped Monica's chin and grazed her cheek with his thumb as he stared into the endless sea green eyes that mirrored the ocean that could be heard from the open window. "I love you," he said as he pulled her down to lie beside him on the fur carpet. "I love you so much, Charles," she said as a single tear slid down her cheek.

Reaching up, Charles wiped at his shoulder. Wetness, his shoulder was wet. He raised his fingers and touched the moisture with the tip of his tongue. Curiosity marred his face, it was salty, like tears. But how? Clenching his fist, Charles turned over and started pounding the blanket over and over.

"Stop the tricks! I don't need this. What more do you want of me?"

It took about ten minutes for him to stop taking out his frustration on the innocent coverings. His mind was playing tricks. Too many days in the dark with only one candle a day that only gave enough light for about one hour and it was left when his meal was brought.

Fresh air, that's what he needed. If he could just get a little air then everything would be all right. Air, food, light and Monica, that's all he wanted. He was dying and he knew it. How much longer he could hold out he did not know, but he would try. He would escape and that was all there was to it, or die trying. What more did he have to lose!

"My, my, my...that was a lovely wedding," Charles heard about the same time as the door that led into the room opened.

Charles did not change his position. He kept his face buried in the blanket and did not even look up to acknowledge his presence. Every so often Jack would appear, taunt him about something new or give him newspapers, informing him about every little change in the town from his funeral to Mrs. Jameson's new baby boy. The last news update he had been given was from the church announcing the engagement of Monica to Jeff. Naturally, that had to be fake for Monica would not even have married this soon after his death, so he had just thrown that paper out through the cage doors where it still lay motionless.

"Don't you want to know what happened? For a few minutes there everyone in the church thought she would refuse but after Jeff coaxed her she agreed. It was exciting for those few moments." Jack gave a little snorted laugh remembering back.

"Too bad she'll have to die soon. He loves her so much and it's a real shame. Are you listening to me or did you die yet?"

"I am just fine. Don't concern yourself over me," Charles smartly replied. "You're just waiting for me to starve to death, so why do you even visit. You could just lock the door and never come back for all I care."

"Well, it is true that I didn't expect you to live this far, what with no food and all. You are more resilient than I had thought."

No food, what did he mean. If he was not the one ordering the meals then who was bringing him food and why? Fascination blossomed in his mind. Who would betray this man's orders? If the person actually had a heart and couldn't let a man starve to death then maybe he could be reasoned with.

"I have just, well, come to like talking to you. It is kind of soothing to me to have someone to talk to and not have anyone overhear us." Jack walked up to the bars and looked down at Charles. He had lost weight and it did seem though that he should be farther gone than what he is. Maybe it was his good health that he had before he was locked in, but he wouldn't last much longer and soon he was going to fill in the stairway to cover his tracks. He would have to put his unwilling assistant in here with her love, buried alive for all time.

"I was thinking, maybe it's time I tell you why I did this. After all, it's not like you can tell anyone and I have needed to talk about it."

"Don't bother bearing your soul. To me you are no more than one sick son-of-a-bitch and if I could reach you I would relieve you of your miserable myself."

Ignoring the insult, Jack removed his coat and sat down on the bottom step in the open doorway.

"You know when a women is wronged it is always left up to the man to make things right. How ironic, men are usually the ones that caused the problem that another has to fix." Jack paused to see if any response was forthcoming. "Well, as I was saying, " he said continuing.

"My mother was wronged. Another women had entered into my father's life and he spent all his money on his whore, leaving my mother in poverty and having to fend for herself when she was pregnant." Jack stood up and started to pace as Charles had done earlier. "How to say the rest? She made her way in life with odd jobs. She would wash clothes, clean houses, and watch other children. She was a good woman and didn't deserve the life she was handed and it nearly killed her till I was old enough to make my own way and provide for her."

"Oh my heart bleeds for you," Charles replied snidely. "Is this going somewhere?"

"Just listen," Jack growled out. Composing himself, Jack straightened his jacket and picked up where he had left off. "I came into manhood and was already trained in strategy and could shoot and ride better than anyone my own age. She made sure I received the best education and saw to it that I was entered into society. She saved every penny so that when I was old enough I could purchase my own company and be respectable, but I always knew why she did it. I was to exact revenge on the one man who took everything from us." Jack stopped and looked through the bars to see if his guest was paying attention. Seeing Charles looking at him now he continued.

"William Morris' wife was the women who captured my fathers attention and he was with her the night that William had come home and found them together. He murdered both of them! They are both still locked up in the home that was made into their coffin. Neither one was ever given a proper funeral."

Grabbing the bars of the cage, Jack shook the bars. "This cage was meant for him and it's a shame that he will never see it."

"If this cell was made for William Morris then why am I in here instead of him?" Charles inquired a little more respectfully this time.

"Well, you see, Jeff murdered him and stole my rightful vengeance. I was outside the house the day it happened. He robbed me of my birthright. It was my duty to end that man's life and it was pulled from under my feet."

Charles sat up and looked quizzically up at Jack. "If the man is dead and your revenge could not be fulfilled then why am I in here?"

Jack turned and sat back down. "You see. I contacted my mother and told her what had happened and she told me that it was my duty to take out the revenge on the son for robbing me of what I was trained to do. I tried to tell her that it was over but she would not hear me. I love her so much and the anguish in her voice told me that she would not be appeased until revenge was exacted, so I planned the rest out. I was there when your wife was brought in and cared for by Jeff and I continued to watch and get updates from my wife Jenny, she is Jeff's cook."

"So, what pulled me into your sick plan?"

"You see, Jeff would sneak into Monica's room at night and watch her. He would pleasure himself at her bedside, then one night I watched as he took advantage of her while she was drugged."

Jack paused as Charles jumped to his feet and came at the bars, just to be brought down to his knees as the chains reached their max limit and tripped him.

"You bastard! You watched him and didn't stop him? What kind of sick freak are you?"

"Well, despite your ranting, it was just what I needed. This untouchable man had a weakness, your wife. I knew that if all went well then I could hurt him more than just physically. I planned it so perfectly, with Monica pregnant and you dead then Jeff would take advantage of the situation thinking she was carrying his child. Jeff would not be able to stand back and not go after her. He always achieved what he wanted and he wanted your wife. I just left the door open for him and he walked right in."

"So, now I am slowly dying because you are playing puppet master and running your little play. What are you going to do about Monica and Jeff?" Hope blossomed in his chest that it was not Monica that he was going to exact his revenge next.

"Well, I hadn't decided yet if I'll wait till the baby is born or not but she is going to have to die. It's the only way to hurt him first. Make him hurt inside like I did when he took my revenge from me." Jack buried his head in his hands as he continued.

"I figured that she is going to have a drowning accident. There is this fountain in Jeff's backyard that she seems to be very fond of and she goes out every night alone and sits by the side of it. I was thinking about arranging a drowning. If her head were under water than I wouldn't have to look her in the face. I never killed a woman and the thought does not give me pleasure at all, but knowing that it's going to kill Jeff seeing her that way will make up for my actions."

Panic leapt through Charles body. "Not Monica, please. She has never done anything to anyone. She helps people out and has never hurt anyone."

"Oh, such a loving soul that she would marry so soon after your funeral. That's really a loving wife with a good soul," he said, mockingly.

"If she remarried it would have been against her wishes or she was coerced. You said yourself that everyone thought for a few moments that she would not go through with it until Jeff said something to her. He has to be holding something over her." Charles tried reasoning.

"I am sorry that she is involved, but if Jeff had not set his eyes on her you would not be in this situation. He killed William, he coveted your wife and he will die, but not before he hurts like I hurt. I planned my whole life, my whole life," he repeated, "in search of the bastard that killed my father and when I find him the opportunity slips through my fingers like grains of sand and I was incapable of stopping the flow as I am incapable of stopping the momentum of what is to come."

Jack stood up and turned his back to Charles. "I am really sorry for you and your wife, but I have to do this." Bending down to get his coat, he glanced over and saw Charles staring at him. If he hadn't been so sure of the cell he had created he would have been afraid of the look in Charles' eyes. He could almost see his own death reflected in the depths. Without saying another word Jack shut the door as he ascended the staircase.

Charles watched as he turned and left. He had to get out of here and one way or another it was going to be soon. He would retain his strength if he had to eat the bugs in the ground to get the sustenance he would need to kill him before Monica could be harmed.

Chapter 41

Congressman Sanders rushed out of the telegraph office with another communication in hand. The yellow paper fluttered in the wind as he rushed back to his office. Normally, no one really took notice anymore, it was normal to see either Jon Sanders or Benjamin Raley rushing from the telegraph office and even more so in the last three weeks, but this time, the slamming door of the telegraph office door made passerby's head swivel in that direction. Sanders had run from the building and had jumped from the wood porch without putting one foot on the steps and without breaking his running pace. The motion made the townsfolk stop and shake their heads at the outrageous behavior.

Jon did not stop till he was in Town Hall, "Sarah," he shouted excitedly. "Sarah, sound the bell. Call everyone in ear shot to a town meeting."

Sarah stood immobile, staring at Jon. This man who barely moved or did anything for that matter was picking up his office, moving the curtains aside and doing it all with a smile and humming to himself. She had never seen him like this before. He was like a new man. A stranger had appeared right before her eyes.

Jon was moving his chair from one side of the desk to the other. He was so excited he couldn't make up his mind if he wanted direct sunlight or shade on him for his speech.

"Which side of the window, humm," Jon said out loud as he looked up at Sarah. She was just standing there with a half smile and let out a little giggle.

"What are you waiting for? Sound the bell and send someone for Benjamin Raley. Now Sarah. hurry... shoo, shooo," he said waving her off with the slight motion of his hand.

Jon turned to his stand and retrieved a very thick file. It contained all of the correspondents with the courts, lawyers, and doctors who evaluated the case. He set the file on his desk and gave his chair one last adjustment. He sat down and closed his eyes to calm himself. It was done. Everything that they had fought for had finally come full circle.

Ding, ding, ding. The sound of the bell ringing finally roused him from his thoughts and he smiled to himself. The last time the bells had rung is when they claimed the epidemic was finally over. It seemed an eternity since that day. It had been one and a half years since the last body was burned and no other symptoms appeared anywhere. Next week would be the fifth anniversary of the day that the town was put in quarantine. It all started with one family that was afflicted with the illness and swept through to the closest neighbors. The illness did not travel quickly like they had expected. It lingered and took its time. By the time the town was put under quarantine, fifteen families and been struck down.

This town came together in its time of grief. Some families were completely wiped out, while others only lost one or two at the most. Orphans were taken in, elderly were cared for by others. Bartering became a way of paying for items and sometimes survival. For those who had money, life was easier than the rest, but money itself really was not of much use except to the greedy. For those who had a skill that was needed it was their ticket to survival and those who did not have a trade, servitude kept them alive.

Like Sarah, she lost both parents and had no skills. Jon had been introduced to her when he came to the town and had been introduced to her father. She was only fifteen when she was orphaned and Jon took pity on her, giving her a job as his secretary, which she excelled at. She ran that office more efficiently than he ever could. She worked hard and never missed a day and was always dependable. He had been the acting mayor for the course of five years since Mayor Jameson succumbed to the illness during that horrid time. Now just thinking about his future the town would need another mayor and maybe she would be just the person to fill his shoes, if he can convince the town to let a woman do the job.

He knew this would change everything now. He watched over two towns and many families that were spread out away from the main areas. Over the years, life had taken on a semblance of normalcy and now it was all about to change. The announcement that he was going to make in a few minutes would change everything. The timing could not be more perfect. The war just ended. The south had succumbed to the north and the president had just signed the declarations that would end the fighting for good. In a way he was glad that Charles was no longer with them to hear that news, after all he was a confederate soldier. The news would have broken his heart.

Ben stood in the doorway watching Jon's features change. It reminded him of watching a child view the changing of seasons. It was amusing to see this side of his friend. Clearing his throat a little louder than what was actually needed, he brought Jon out of his musings.

"So, do I need to ask?" Ben quarried, cocking his head sideways.

"We won, Ben. We won," Jon sighed. "I can go home to my children, you to your wife and the town will blossom again with trade and new money coming in from visitors. The patrols will be called off this week."

Ben walked over to the desk and sank down into the high back leather chair. All of the information was sinking in. "It's really over," he stated.

"We could never have done it without your help. Thank you."

Ben didn't look up. He had not seen his wife since he arrived here the same day as Jon. The same day the patrols were posted and the quarantine signs were set up and the boundaries were staked. He survived just as Jon had done as well as Dr. Jeninson, but five others that were in the entourage never made it. The illness had taken many lives. Life was a mystery. Fate had a cruel way of stepping in. He was the only one that had any type of law training in the area and Jeninson was the only doctor here as well.

It took a Congressman acting as mayor, a lawyer, and a retired doctor to finally clear the town and gain it's freedom. The strangest thing was that none of them were actually from the area. The only consolation is that the war is over and the town breezed through it like nothing ever happened. Half the town doesn't even know the extent of damage that was done. He didn't know if that was a blessing or a curse but soon enough the town would know. He would tell them after Jon gave the news about the quarantine being lifted. The information would devastate most of them, but he was sure the towns' freedom would override the sadness.

"Ben, have you been listening?"

"Oh, sorry, Jon. Thank you, but it was your idea. I guess a celebration is in order."

"The patrols and the Governor are suppose to come through here next Wednesday and hand over the proclamation of freedom to us. We'll hold the celebration that day. We'll declare is Liberation Day. How does that sound?"

"That's a great name. The town will forever remember that day. I'll write up a legal declaration that will make it a formal holiday for both Sandersville and Oak Ridge. These two towns will always be linked and no other place in the country will be able to celebrate that day."

"You know I'll be leaving the day after. What do you think of me appointing Sarah as acting mayor until a vote can be taken."

"Jon, you just keep surprising me. Sarah would be the perfect person and I believe that she would be honored to take the position. No one else in town would be more perfect than her. We just have to convince the council that a woman can do the job."

"Ben, this is Liberation Day. Changes are good for our town, don't you think?"

Hearing whimpers coming from the doorway, both men looked up to see Sarah standing there. Tears were streaming down her face and her hands were overlapped, covering her mouth. Both men ceased the conversation and went over to the distraught girl.

"Sarah," Jon said gathering her into his arms. "I was hoping to ask you first. I didn't mean to spring this on you."

Jon tightened his arms around her and she slumped over in his embrace. He tried to comfort her the best he knew how. Sarah laid her head on his chest. Her tears soaked the lapel of his jacket, leaving dark stains and the tears flowed.

"I didn't know it would stress you so much to be nominated. I'll find someone else if that would make you happy."

"Sir, I am honored that you would nominate me for mayor. That is the greatest honor that I've ever been offered and I am grateful that you would entrust that position to me, I really am." Sarah paused as she pulled away and pulled a hanky out from her sleeve and dabbed at her tears. She waited to continue till she had composed herself again.

"I just… well…" She stopped again to control her voice. "You're the closest person I have to what I would call family. I lost everyone and if you leave, well, then I won't have anyone." With that said, she lowered her head as another torrent of tears followed in the wake of the others.

"Sarah, listen to me. I will always love you like a daughter and I have watched you grow and mature. This town needs you and everyone here is family. You will be there for them, just like they will be there for you. Don't ever forget that." Jon gently placed a kiss on her forehead.

"Now, let's dry those tears and break the news. You don't want your extended family seeing you cry now do you."

Jon and Ben gave Sarah time to compose herself again before turning towards the window and looking into all the expectant faces. Taking a deep breath, Jon approached the window first. It was time.

Chapter 42

Charles lay on his wool blanket, his legs crossed and his head rested in his hands. Staring into the blackness was soothing. It gave him time to think and to plan. He knew three days had passed since he was told about the plot that had unfolded around him. All he wanted to do was get to Monica. He had to get to her and protect her. If Jack had his way then all hope would be lost and Monica and the baby would parish.

Light broke through his revelry as the door opened that led to the staircase. Charles lightly turned when the sound of footsteps coming down the stairs could be heard. The creaking of the door echoed in the small room as the hinges screamed in protest. Charles normally didn't even look over at the exit. Jack had been in so many times to boast about the impending murder that Charles didn't even care what the man had to say anymore. But, still something was different. Usually there was boasting the minute the door opened, but this time there was silence.

Yellow billowing lace could be seen through the open door. The material swished around quickly and then back again as if waiting on someone. It must certainly be a woman, she would take one step and then stop, look back, then proceed to go forward again before turning back again.

Charles didn't even get up. This had become a very boring game and he had no interest in playing today. He decided that he would just pretend to be asleep or try to play dead and just maybe they would go away.

"Charles?"

That's a new one, he thought to himself. Sneak attack, have the woman approach him. These mind games were getting old and besides he was to weak to even pay attention to them.

"Charles, wake up, it's Suzanne."

"Suzanne!" Charles exclaimed excitedly. "How did you find me?" he continued as he tried to sit up.

"That's not important. What is important is that I have to get you out of here. Jack is on his way to Jeff's. He was just going to leave you here to die. I cannot permit that," Suzanne hurriedly remarked as she pulled the key to the cage door from the folds of her skirt.

Hearing the click of the cage door lock, he glanced up at her. Where did she get the key? Realization dawned on him. It was her that stood there that day and not Monica, but why was she helping that maniac. The how's and why's really didn't matter. What did matter was the fact that one more door was open to him, if he could just convince her to release the ankle bracelet then he could escape. He had to convince her.

"Why did you help him, Suzanne? I know it was you with him on those minute occasions."

Suzanne paused and bowed her head as she closed her eyes. She left the cage door shut as she leaned her head against the cold steel bars as tears formed in her eyes. She only glanced up a moment when she heard rustling coming from the cell. The light from the open door behind her only let in enough light to illuminate only one corner of the room that held her love. She strained her eyes to see into the corner where Charles was, but it was just to dark to see him clearly.

Charles' legs screamed in protest as he rose up onto his knees. All the days of little or no motion had stiffened every muscle and joint in his legs.

"Suzanne?" Charles beseeched gently. "Why didn't you tell someone I was here?"

Just hearing the concern in Charles voice was more than she could take, sinking down to the ground, sobs racked her body as she allowed the tears to come freely.

"I wanted..." Her voice caught in her throat. She couldn't say it.

"Wanted what, honey? You can tell me," he inquired further. He purposely kept his voice calm.

"I wanted you..." Came the timid response.

The words were spoken so softly though he almost thought he didn't hear her correctly. His eyes widened in astonishment at hearing the quit confession. Realization sank even deeper and hit him like a boulder. All the smiles, her giddiness, her body motion, all the times they had been in a room together and she would move closer to him. Scene after scene played through his mind. Finally he understood. All this time she had hidden feelings.

Charles' jaw twitched as the thought of her betrayal. Her hidden feelings had kept him prisoner. Had kept him away from Monica and from his freedom. Anger, pain and rage roared inside of him. Hatred for this pitiful woman built up and threatened to pour over. Taking a deep breath, he calmed himself and reminded himself to keep a clear head until he was free, then he would deal with her personally. Charles mentally prepared himself and softened the tone of his voice.

"Oh Suzanne, I didn't know. Why didn't you tell me?"

Slowly raising her head she peered at Charles through the bars of the cage. He was sitting up in the lighted area and was looking at her. His eyes looked so sad, his features were so drawn out and his lips formed a deep frown.

"Suzanne, it was Monica wasn't it? Your friendship with her is what stopped you wasn't it?"

She began to weep uncontrollably now and her shoulders shook with the force of them. She buried her tear stained face into the crook of her arm as the rested against the bars once more.

Charles strained to reach out towards Suzanne in a fake attempt to touch her. He knew he could not reach her. The chain attached to his ankle never allowed him to get closer than two feet from the bars, but she didn't know that.

"Come to me," Charles implored of her. He didn't even attempt to rise from his kneeling position. He needed to make her come to him.

Startled by the soft, yet demanding offer, she stood up and threw open the cage door and rushed into the open arms that were now extended to welcome her.

Charles incased her in his arms and smiled outwardly as she buried her face into the crook of his neck. He pulled back lightly and raised her chin up, he looked deeply into her eyes then claimed her mouth with his. He felt her body yield to him and knew he had won. It would not be long now and he would be free.

Revolt and shame filled his mind and his senses, but he wanted to play this to it's fullest. He swallowed the bile that arose in his throat as he released her lips to smother kisses upon her face and trailed them down her neck. He allowed his hands to roam her petite figure of their own free will. She inhaled sharply at the feel of his hand on her ample bosom, kneading it gently into submission.

Delirium and want heated her every pore. Pulsations and wanton lust sprang to life in her most intimate regions as his hands worked its magic on her body. Light moans escaped her lips as Charles unbuttoned her dress. Tears started spilling over, but this time they were tears of pleasure. She had wanted, no desired this for so long. Her body demanded more and had needed this ever since she had first met him. She allowed him to lower the top of her gown and sighed as he untied the corset beneath. As the restraining material was thrown aside, tiny shivers shot through her body as the feel of his wet lips covered her breasts. Her nipples became erect and seemed to have a life of their own as they strained to be touched.

Charles knew what she wanted and he would play this role thoroughly, Monica's life depended on it. "Please forgive me," he silently pleaded in his mind as his thoughts went to his love.

He lowered her carefully to the ground, making sure she was close enough to the cage that he could not continue this tryst. The last of her garments were thrown to the side so that she lay naked in front of him. He ran his fingers up her thigh and lingered long enough on her intimate region just long enough to feel her shudder. He lowered his breeches and rose up and went to cover her.

"Damn it," he shouted.

Startled, Suzanne glanced up to see Charles looking back. She followed his line of sight to the chain that was pulled taught. Frantic with passion, she quickly stood up and raced to the stairwell. There on the step was a chisel and hammer along with a knife that she had brought with her. Looking at the knife, she pushed it to the side. It was not needed, that she was sure of. Picking up the hammer and chisel she raced back to Charles who was frantically pulling at the chain.

Charles reached up and took the tools and started pounding at the offensive shackle. It took several attempts but the chain fell away. He was free. Charles jumped up and stood in front of Suzanne. "You bitch!" he shouted reaching out and grabbed Suzanne by the throat. With renewed energy, Charles threw her to the side. "I should kill you for what you have done to Monica and I, but I think I'll leave you here to rot in your own soil."

Just to prove his point, he kicked some of the loose dirt from the ground onto her and turned and refastened his pants as he walked out of the cage and into the sunlight.

Suzanne glared at him. She had been tricked. He would pay for that. She raced to the stairwell and picked up the knife that she had left lying there and looked up to see him exit the doorway above. With no regards to her undressed form she raced after him. Her eyes blazed angrily as she watched him trying to mount her horse. She raised the knife and plunged it into Charles shoulder. Hearing him yell out, she stepped back and withdrew the knife as he fell back.

Hitting the ground hard, Charles reached back to try and find out why his shoulder had begun to throb. He felt around with his hand and came into contact with a sticky liquid. Bringing his hand around so that he could see it, blood covered his fingers. He spun around and faced his attacker. She was slightly bent at the waist and still held the blood soaked dagger in her hand. He knew that the outcome was not going to be good for him or her.

"Suzanne, you have to stop this. Can't you see that we are not meant to be."

Just as he said that, she jabbed out again and this time his tender flesh of his right side felt the insertion of the deadly weapon. He immediately jumped in the opposite direction and covered the open wound.

"Suzanne," He frantically shouted as he leaped out of the way as she struck out again.

"You think you can seduce me and then run back to her. She doesn't want you, can't you see that," she screamed at him as she tried to circle him.

He anticipated her moves and kept eye contact with her as he turned with her. He had to end this. Without warning he leapt at her and grabbed her arm. With her good arm still free, she embedded the knife into his unprotected abdomen. Charles inhaled deeply as he cringed but kept his hold on her. He reached over with his free hand and pulled the deeply entrenched dagger out and turned it on her. She fell to her knees, her eyes wide as she looked down at the knife sticking out of her chest just below her left breast. She inhaled once more before her lifeless body fell to the ground.

Charles looked down and kicked her body with his foot to make sure it was over then turned back to the awaiting horse. He held his abdomen to try and stop the bleeding as he mounted the animal. The wound was deep and would need mending, but he didn't have time. He jabbed the animal into a fierce gallop.

Chapter 43

Congressman Sanders and Dr. Jeninson were outside of town hall and were waiting the arrival of the Governor. He was coming four days sooner than planned. The patrols were already pulled away and the town's people lined the streets. This day was anticipated but when the messenger arrived with the news it was a shock to all of them.

"What a day for this. I had to Leave Monica Morris with a midwife to be here," Dr. Jeninson stated flatly. "I would actually prefer to be birthing babies than talking politics."

"I know, but we needed you here. The towns people and the Governor will want to thank the men that gave them back their freedom," Congressman Sanders stated soundly. He was not going to let anything spoil this day.

"Rider coming," shouted the Deputy as he raced up to town hall.

"Everyone prepare yourselves. It's probably the scout, that means he is around the bend."

Not a sound was heard as everyone stood nearby and waited in anticipation for the rider to come through. Galloping could be heard before the rider was actually seen. The figure was slumped over the saddle horn as the horse halted in front of town hall. Dr. Jeninson ran over and yelled for assistance to take the injured man down. The man was shirtless and had several wounds on his upper torso. Calling for his bag he started to bandage the wounds there on the street to staunch the flow of blood. He carefully wiped at this mans face, clearing dirt and blood away. As he was finishing up, the stranger's eyes opened.

"My god. Charles."

Dr. Jeninson called out to the Congressman. "Jon, get down here. Fast!"

"There's no time," Charles said through his parched lips. "Get me to Jeff Morris' house please."

"You're wounded. If we don't stop this blood you will bleed to death." Looking up, Dr. Jeninson noticed that Jon knew exactly who was on the ground, but he did not stop his administrations until he was sure that every wound had been bandaged.

"We have to go. Monica is in danger. He's going to kill her," Charles stated as he tried to get up. Falling back, he looked up at the doctor. "Help me to your carriage. I'll explain on the way."

Jon and the doctor looked at each other worriedly, but did as requested. They requested assistance from some of the men folk that had gathered for the governor's arrival and had Charles placed into the carriage. They followed closely behind and just as soon as he was comfortable, they seated themselves. Dr. Jeninson gave his driver orders to be careful, but also to get them to the Morris' residence as soon as possible.

As the carriage started moving, Charles poured out what had transpired over the last few months, omitting nothing.

Jack lay in wait. He had heard the screams coming from the second story window and new the babe must be on its way. He sat down and waited from below. The bushes concealing his presence again, just like they did a hundred times before. It seemed like an eternity had passed before he heard the wail of the newborn. Looking up at the window he felt relief wash over him. He had no wish to harm an innocent baby and the birth gave him the freedom to execute his revenge without harming anyone else than was necessary. He listened for several more minutes before going around back and entering the house.

Jeff had followed the nursemaid into the nursery as Monica rested. The babe was a welcome addition. His son was finally here. The child's hair was dark like his mothers and his eyes were the dark blue that all babes had, but he was sure they would turn the lighter shade of blue like his own. He stood back as the nurse gave the babe his first bath and prepared him to greet his mother properly.

The scene was a little too touching for Jack's liking, so he excused himself from the scene quickly before he had any second thoughts. He quickly looked back to make sure that he had not been seen, then carefully opened the door to the birthing room. There in the middle of the large bed, Monica slept. She was already pail and looked weak. He lowered his eyes to the ground as he made his way over to her. Without taking a second thought, he covered her nose and mouth with his hand and leaned down on her so that she could not move. He pinned her arms in place with his body and pressed hard on her chest.

Monica's eyes opened abruptly and panic set in. She couldn't breath and it felt like she was being crushed. She looked straight into the face of the man that held her down. She knew that face. But what was he doing? Why couldn't she breath? Her lungs started burning and her eyes watered. Her throat started to swell slightly from the pressure and her eyes rolled back. She started to kick out and tried to wiggle away from the mans hold. It seemed the more she fought the tighter he held her. Monica watched as he looked away and lowered his head, but he did not release his grasp. Monica remembered where she had seen him. The store, the store, that was the last thought that crossed her mind as she blacked out.

Jack held his position for a while longer, knowing that just passing out did not mean that your life was completely gone. He wanted to make sure the deed was done correctly. After a few more minutes passed, he turned back and looked at her. He had never looked upon a woman as she died before. It seemed as if she was still sleeping. He lowered his ear to her chest and made sure that no heartbeat could be detected. When he was sure the first part was complete he released her and stood up. He straightened her blankets and smoothed them down and ran his fingers through her hair and laid her arms down by her sides. Now, for the finale. Jack walked around the bed and opened the door that joined the master bedroom to this one and there he waited.

He didn't have long though. Jeff walked in and glanced over at Monica. She was so beautiful, even in her sleep she was peaceful looking. She didn't stir as he sat down on the bed next to her. He new she needed rest, it had been a stressful birth. Reaching over he smoothed her hair away from her face and stared down at her. He had everything he could ever want, a child and a beautiful wife and right now he just wanted to hold her. Jeff leaned down and rested his head on her chest. He became frozen in place, she didn't seem to be breathing.

"Monica, wake up," he said, shaking her gently. "Monica?" he shouted and then started to shake her more forcefully.

"Mrs. Thomas, get the nurse. Something's wrong with Monica."

The nurse rushed into the room and checked Monica over. She listened for any breathing sounds then checked for a heartbeat. She looked up at Jeff and slowly shook her head. "I am sorry sir, she's gone."

Jeff kneeled next to the bed and laid his head on the edge. "Get out!"

Both women left the room and closed the door. As they turned to walk towards the baby's room they were stopped in their tracks. Jeff's anguished scream echoed through the halls of the manor followed by wailing sobs. The women looked at each other and lowered their eyes to the ground. Tears formed in Mrs. Thomas' eyes as she walked into the nursery. She had just lost the only daughter she ever had.

Eyes danced with laughter as they watched the scene unfold in front of them. Jack watched as Jeff took Monica's hand and raised it to his tear stained face and kissed it. A small part of him was saddened that he was the one that ended her life, but the other side of him rejoiced in the agony that he had inflicted on this man. He wanted to stay and watch the pain he had inflicted on this man, but the sound of a carriage racing up the drive was heard through the open window. Damn, he swore to himself. Company was not in his plans. Now he would have to rush in order to escape from here, but first there was one more task to complete.

Pulling out the pistol that he had stolen a year ago, he slipped back through the door and into the room with Jeff. He stood motionless for a few more seconds, looking over the scene, before letting his presence be known.

Jeff peered over and jumped up, never taking his eyes off of the pistol pointed in his direction. He steadied himself and looked up at the intruder.

"Jack, what are you doing here?" Jeff demanded.

"Taking care of business. If you wouldn't mind turning around and kneeling down for me."

Jack didn't move. He didn't want to get close enough for this man to have a chance to spring any surprise attack. He knew better than to let this man have any kind of advantage. He was just as ruthless as himself.

"Why are you doing this? We're friends and look," Jeff said pointing to the bed. "I just lost my wife. Don't you even care?"

Jack didn't even peer at the bed as he ordered Jeff to do as told again and this time he raised the pistol to let him know that this was no joke.

"Do you really want to know what happened to her? I put her out of her misery. I couldn't let you die without suffering first like I am."

"What the hell are you talking about? Why would you want me to suffer?" Jeff asked as he turned around and kneeled down.

"I wish I had more time to explain things out to you, but we have unexpected company and I really don't have time for a lengthy explanation. Just remember that before you kill someone, make sure no one else wants to do it first." Hearing footsteps coming up the stairs, Jack knew his time was limited. Without further explanation he pulled the trigger. The gunshot echoed through the small room right before the door was thrown open.

Congressman Sanders was the first through the door. He glanced over the sight before him. Jeff lie on the ground, bleeding profusely from his head, Monica lay on the bed and Jack was standing in the room loading his gun. Just as the doctor entered the room another shot echoed through the room, startling the two men. Jack collapsed just a few moments afterwards, adding more blood to the already stained carpet. Jon looked away and tried to get out of the room before his stomach lost its contents, but the sight of Charles slowly climbing the stairs cleared his head.

"Don't go in, Charles. You don't want to see what's in there," he said putting a hand on Charles' arm, trying to stop him.

Charles pushed his way past him and stumbled into the room. Seeing Jeff's body on the floor had no affect on him, but when he saw Monica laying on the bed his heart sank and his breath caught in his throat. Weakened from blood loss and on the brink of passing out, he shook his head to clear his thoughts. He stumbled over to the bed as if in a dream. His sight was becoming cloudy and he didn't know how much longer he could keep his thoughts clear. He managed to reach the bed and lifted Monica just enough so he could sit beside her and hold her in his arms.

Tears streamed down his face as he smoothed her hair back away from her face, knowing she was already gone, he leaned down and placed a kiss on her lips. He laid back and leaned her against his chest as he cradled her head in his arms. He rocked her gently before laying his head next to hers.

Jon and Dr. Jeninson watched as Charles became motionless, holding his wife in his arms. Both men turned and walked out the door. This was the saddest day in the history of these towns. Dr. Jeninson closed the door as he lowered his head and Jon slid to the floor as a lone tear slipped down his cheek.

"Some Liberation Day."

Printed in the United States
77714LV00002B/121